CLAIMING THEIR FOREVER

A FERAL BREED ANTHOLOGY

ELLIS LEIGH

Kinship Press

Claiming Their Forever
Copyright ©2015 by Ellis Leigh
All rights reserved
ISBN: 978-0-9961465-0-0

Kinship Press
P.O. Box 221
Prospect heights, IL 60070

Edited by Silently Correcting Your Grammar, LLC
Cover Design by Cormar Covers

For my family,
Without you, I'd have nothing.

CLAIMING THEIR FOREVER

Rebel & Charlotte

November: Takes Place During Chapter #18 of *Claiming His Witch*

Rebel

We trudged back to the cabin, following Pup and Azurine the whole way. Those two were practically celebrating in the woods while Charlotte and I stayed silent. Fuck, what a mess this night had been. I would never have expected Spook to go feral, though fighting him off wouldn't have been a big deal normally. But I'd been distracted. Knowing my mate and another Breed member's mate were a few feet away had made it difficult to focus on the fight.

And then Pup.

Just the barest hint of that memory swirling in my head and I felt sick. I'd seen Breed members die before, been by their side as they passed on, either from aging or battle. But tonight had been different. Pup was special to us. The blood of two respected members ran through his veins: Gates, who'd saved his life after the fiasco in Milwaukee, and Beast, his wolf-giver. Pup was honest, hard-working, and had a drive rarely seen anymore. I didn't just like Pup; I respected him.

Watching him die had taken a few decades off my life, I was sure.

When we reached the cabin, I directed Charlotte inside. No

long goodbyes to the other couple or promises to see each other later. I knew Pup and Azurine would be busy reconnecting tonight. A man doesn't fight off death without a shit-ton of adrenaline coursing through his veins. Pup was gonna crash—and hard.

But I had faith Azurine could deal with her mate. As I could deal with mine. Charlotte was shaking and pale, with no expression on her face. I worried she was going into shock, so I helped her out of her coat and boots and turned up the heat to keep her warm. And then I stood there…helpless and frustrated, my body trembling as my own adrenaline levels dropped.

Fuck, we'd lost Pup tonight. Not almost, not close call. He'd been dead. I still had no idea what exactly worked to bring him back, but I was grateful. And terrified at how close we'd come to tragedy.

"Is that how it always is?" Charlotte whispered, her voice shaky. It was enough to pull me from my thoughts of death.

I spun in her direction. "What?"

She peered up at me, face blank, the blue eyes I loved so much empty and almost soulless. "Fighting…death. Is your world always so violent?"

My mouth fell open, but I closed it again with a snap. I had no idea what to say. Refusal would be a lie, and yet it wasn't *always* so brutal. Tonight had been particularly harsh for all of us. A nightmare playing out while we were awake.

When I didn't answer, she shook her head, returning her gaze to the floor. "How can you live like that? How can you expect me to?"

I swallowed hard, my heart breaking and my head thumping. Fuck, we'd just reached a good place in our relationship. I'd finally broken through her trust issues and fear, gotten her to open up to me and be willing to accept my place in her life. I couldn't bear to see those walls going back up.

I'd hidden a lot of things regarding wolves and the Breed from her, thinking she couldn't handle the reality of my world. But seeing Pup die and watching the miracle that was his rebirth had reminded me how short our lives were, even those of us who lived for centuries. I couldn't hold back, not again. She'd left me once and broken my heart… If she did it again, it'd kill me.

Slowly, as if stalking prey, I slunk down to the floor and sat in front of her.

"When I was young, the weight of a man's word meant everything. Contracts were a rarity, so you had to learn to trust your instincts about people." I paused, reaching for her hand to feel her near me. "My father taught me to look men in the eye when we were dealing, to shake hands on the deal, and to always meet my end of the bargain. That way a man knew I was trustworthy. And when I was turned and joined the world of shifters, those lessons stayed with me.

"The winter I joined the Feral Breed, I was traveling through the northern part of the country. I was alone, lonely, and falling fast to the lure of the feral side of our nature. Wolves don't do well alone, kitten. Ever."

She nodded, her eyes coming alive as they stayed locked on mine.

"I came across a pack along the Rocky Mountain Front and requested permission to stay for a few days. It's not unusual for roaming single wolves to do this—it provides the possibility of increasing the pack size should the guest discover his mate."

I ran a finger over her face, still so fucking thankful I'd found her at all. She tilted her head into my touch and kissed my palm, making me smile.

"Are you warm enough?" I asked. She nodded, so I took a deep breath and let myself sink back into my memories.

"The pack was traditional, which means a lot of the rules were, to me, cruel. Not long after I arrived, the Alpha banished a group of men. Young male shifters who'd known no other life than that pack, sent out into the wild with nothing but their clothes and whatever trinkets they carried as mementos. See, there're never enough females in a traditional pack. Shewolves are a bit rare, and unless the pack chooses to integrate with the human world, there's very little chance to find a woman to be with."

"You mean to find a mate."

I sighed. "No, not just find a mate. Some wolves give up looking for their other half and simply claim a partner as theirs. It's more like a human marriage. They stay together through the human's lifespan, have children, take care of one another."

"Why wouldn't the pack just turn some human women?" she asked. My blood ran cold, ancient words taught to me since the moment I'd woken up a shifter blaring through my head.

"We do not turn women. Ever."

I sighed as she looked at me with wide eyes, but I couldn't be distracted by that tangent. The danger of giving women the turning bite would have to be shelved for another day.

"Back to the pack." I raised my eyebrows as she gave me an irritated look. "To keep the male leaders happy, and to keep the Alpha satisfied, young men are kicked out and the women are…" I paused, not sure if I wanted to share this information or not.

But Charlotte refused to let me sugarcoat things. "Tell me."

Her whispered demand made me swallow and grit my teeth as I whispered, "They're not given the choice of partner or person who will be the father of their children."

Her gasp broke my heart, and I squeezed my eyes closed before shaking my head.

"I don't believe in that. None of us in the Breed believes in that. Our leader, Blaze, has been fighting to change the old ways for decades." I leaned in, capturing her attention and holding her gaze. "Every person should be able to consent to his or her coupling. Period."

She paused then nodded, her eyes watery and her face pale. I squeezed her hand, making sure our connection to each other was strong.

"One of the males being forced out was a boy named Teddy. He was only six years old. When I questioned one of the pack leaders about it, I learned the leader of the pack had called Alpha Prerogative on Teddy's mother, meaning he was taking her as his bedmate for the breeding season. The Alpha decided the boy was in the way, so he banished the child."

I blinked back the sting in my eyes as Charlotte did the same. Moving forward, closer, I pressed our knees together and moved my hands to hold her wrists.

"His mother screamed and sobbed the day the boy was escorted off pack land, and the poor boy's tears ran like water. I couldn't take it. My heart broke for that mother and her child. Later that day, I snuck through the camp until I found the den of Teddy's mother. She was still sobbing, unable to leave her bed. Once I found her, I never thought twice about what I needed to do. I hoisted her over my shoulder and raced through the woods until we picked up the trail of the ousted men.

"It took us almost a full day, but we found Teddy, and then the three of us ran like hell. For two months, Alice, Teddy, and I traveled together, dodging their old packmates who'd been sent to hunt for us and avoiding feral wolves as much as we could. Finally, we ended up at a Feral Breed denhouse in Arizona, desperate for a place to stay and hoping they'd offer sanctuary for the mother and child at the least. There, I met Beast, who was working with my friend Jameson to clear up a man-eater issue in the hills. When I explained who we were and why we were running, Beast and Jameson both looked me square in the eye and promised to find us help. And they did. Jameson found Alice and Teddy a pack in northern California, one with more modern rules. The three of us moved them there just a few weeks after showing up on the denhouse doorstep."

Charlotte's eyes were bright, an anxious, excited expression on her face. "What happened to Alice and her son?"

I smiled as I thought about the last time I'd heard from the two. "Alice eventually found her mate. They have four or five children together, if I remember right. Teddy grew up to be a fucking charmer. The boy could talk you into just about anything. He eventually joined the Feral Breed, though he's not in my den."

I inched closer, holding both her hands in mine. "Sometimes, the fights are horrible and ugly like today. But sometimes… sometimes they're so fucking worth it. Alice and Teddy were worth it; you and the other humans at Amnesia were worth it. Hell, even today, fighting to keep Azurine and her sisters safe, that was worth it. Because I refuse to let anyone force their will on another. I refuse to sit back and watch my people and my friends be terrorized or made into victims. I fight so others don't have to. My life isn't all danger and death, though."

I paused, taking a deep breath before I told her the one thing I feared confessing the most. "The Feral Breed is my family. They're my brothers. And I can't leave them after I've promised to be there for them in good times and in bad."

Charlotte closed her eyes and turned her face away. "So if I agree to this life, to exchanging mating bites"—she turned to peer at me with tears in her eyes—"my life gets extended to match yours. I have to watch my brother, my only family, die. And it's quite possible I'll have to watch you die as well?"

I pulled her into my arms, not quite following her logic. "No, baby. I'm strong and healthy. I'm trained to fight and have a team of men backing me up and battling beside me. You won't have to watch me die."

Her choked sob gutted me, but it was her words that sent my mind reeling and nearly turned my world on its side.

"I already did," she practically yelled against me. "I couldn't tell who was who when you were a wolf. I got confused." She sniffled and pulled out of my arms, wiping her face with one shaking hand. "I thought you were the one who'd been killed."

Her words hit me like a blow to the gut. *She'd thought I died.* My mate, the woman who owned my heart, had suffered because she watched a similar-looking wolf fall in battle. My chest ached as I reached for her. I pulled her into my lap and wrapped myself around her, both arms and legs. Pressed together like this, there was no denying my heartbeat or breathing. She'd know for sure I'd made it. That I was still with her. That I was alive.

Charlotte clung to me, her sobs growing louder and rougher as I tried to calm her. But there was no calming her. No balm for the emotional burn she must have felt. All I could do was hold her, show her I was alive and well, and wait for her to work through it enough to talk to me.

But then Charlotte did something that took me by surprise. She arched her back, pressed her hips into mine, and kissed me. Not a peck or a light touch of her lips. No, she owned my mouth and demanded entrance with her tongue. I barely responded, too fearful of upsetting her more to know what to do. But her lips tasted like sugar and she was so warm against me. And when her hands fisted in my hair, I was done.

I rolled her to the floor, stroking her tongue with mine as I settled on top of her. Her hands were needy, almost painful as they clutched and clawed at my arms and back. And I loved it.

Breathing fast, rolling her hips against mine, my woman made a sound like a growl as she bit my lip. "Now, Abraham. Please."

I gave her a silencing, lapping kiss before placing my forehead against hers. "Baby, I want you. I always want you. But are you sure—"

Charlotte opened her eyes and met mine, the pain and anguish so clear in hers, it took my breath away.

"I watched you die. I need this. I need you." Her eyes teared up again, and her hands clutched me closer. "Please."

With a sigh and a sense of something bigger going on here, I whispered okay before taking her mouth once more. Trembling hands made fast work of our clothes. We only separated long enough to remove them before clinging to one another again, Charlotte always pulling me back on top of her.

And when we were naked, tied up in each other in a way that left no part untouched, she gripped my face with both hands and whispered against my lips.

"Never again. I can't live without you. I thought… No. Never again."

My brows furrowed at the evidence of her fear, but she must have noticed my hesitation.

She held my gaze, honest and true, and she whispered, "Make love to me, Abraham. Make me feel something other than fear."

"Kitten." I nuzzled my nose along hers "I don't—"

Charlotte slid her hand between us, cutting off my argument. There was no hesitation in her movements. Within seconds, she gripped me, her fingers circling my cock and bringing me to her pussy.

"I need this." Charlotte kept her eyes on mine, never faltering. Telling the truth. She needed this, us, me. She needed the reconnection.

And I knew I needed to give it to her.

With nothing more than a nod of acceptance, I slid inside her heat, nudging my way back and forth until I was completely seated. She sighed and held me close, her legs around my hips and her arms around my shoulders.

I worked her full and deep, refusing to ease my weight off her body. I kept my pace slow and gentle, filling the silence with soft words of love and comfort. But as the pleasure grew, as Charlotte's breathy gasps and moans came more often, I knew she needed more.

Sitting up, I pulled her into my lap. She slid down my cock, pulling me in deeper as she angled her hips. Moaning, eyes closed, Charlotte leaned back and ground into me. Once, twice, three times…working herself on me until she had a rhythm going that made my eyes roll back in my head.

Fuck, she was so sexy. I pumped into her, my fingers sinking into the flesh of her round hips, the motion making her breasts wiggle in front of my face. I was such a lucky bastard. This gorgeous, ripe woman was beyond my wildest dreams. And she was mine.

When she finally came, with her tilted head back and her body bowed, I followed, knowing our reconnection wasn't complete. Maybe it never would be. We'd spent months going back and forth over being together. Charlotte had trust issues and was completely focused on her brother's care. And I accepted that.

We'd moved slowly, dating, taking Julian with us oftentimes. But things had been looking better before this trip. We'd talked about me moving into her house in Milwaukee. Making a little family of three. And while it wasn't the perfect solution for me, it was what my mate wanted, and I'd give her the world if I could.

I just hoped it was enough.

We clung to one another as our breathing slowed. Hands moved restlessly, mine up and down her back and over her hips, hers along my arms and up my neck. It was as if neither of us could get enough of the other, that we refused to let go.

"Abraham?" The nervousness in Charlotte's voice caught my attention, and I leaned back to meet her tentative gaze. "Will you shift to your wolf, please?"

"Excuse me?" Confusion kept me in my place, frozen. Charlotte had never asked to see my wolf. In fact, I would have bet she was afraid of him. She definitely grew anxious around other shifters, even when they were in their human form. "I don't understand."

"When that other wolf died…" She bit her lip, her eyes growing watery. "I couldn't tell the two of you apart. I thought it was you. I thought you'd died."

I ran my hands up her arms. "But I didn't. I made it; I'm right here."

"Yes, but what about next time?" She shook her head. "If I'm going to be with you, I need to know you. All of you. Both sides of your soul. That means I need to get to know your wolf."

I breathed in, uncertainty slowing my decision. "Charlotte, you don't have to do this. I know that part of me scares you."

She huffed a sarcastic laugh. "Yeah, well…watching you bleed out all over the forest floor scared me more."

I sat stunned, the anger in her voice holding my words hostage. Watching the fight with Spook had affected her more than I'd originally thought. More than I would have wanted. My kitten was pissed and needed to regain some kind of control. And introducing her to my wolf would give it to her. At least in her own mind.

Untangling myself, I stood and took a few steps back. She watched me from her place on the floor, eyes wide and breathing quiet.

"When I'm a wolf, I'm still me," I said. "You don't have to be afraid."

Charlotte sat up, never looking away from my stare. "You'd never hurt me."

I nodded. My heart raced as I took a deep breath. This could either go very well or very badly. But it was what my mate wanted, so I closed my eyes and surrendered to the shift.

Once on all fours, I shook out my coat and met Charlotte's surprised eyes. Whining, tail wagging, I waited for her to give me a signal, some kind of sign that she was ready for me to approach her. Praying all the while that she didn't up and run out of the cabin.

Finally, after staring at me for several minutes, she crawled up onto her knees. I waited as she moved closer, not wanting to frighten her. But when she reached me, when she was close enough to touch, she brought her fingers to my neck and sank them into my fur.

"I thought it was you." She inspected me, her eyes traveling over every inch of my lupine form. "I should have paid more attention. You're a lighter gray than he was."

She petted me slowly, gently learning every dip and curve. I preened under her attention. My tail wagged harder and my muscles clenched as her hands slid over them. I loved her hands on me. And when she used her nails to scratch through my fur, I whined and dropped to the floor, ready to roll over and show her my belly. She just chuckled and kept petting me, scratching my ears, running her fingers over my snout.

After a while, she inched closer, wrapping her arm around my shoulders, hugging me. And then she started to cry.

I shifted to my human form, picking her up and putting her back in my lap as I wrapped myself around her.

"It's okay," I soothed, rocking her subtly. "I'm right here, and it's okay."

My heart broke for her. I couldn't even imagine how much of a wreck I'd be if the situation were reversed. I doubted I'd ever let her out of my sight again. So I held her, and I let her cling to me. And we rocked. For a long time, only the sounds of her crying broke the silence of the cabin. But then she took a deep breath.

"Abraham, what we have…it terrifies me." Her voice was soft and rough from her tears. "If I say yes to forever with you, I'll have to watch my brother die."

"Char, you won't—"

"Yes, I will. Even if it's from old age, I'll have to watch him die. You don't know; you weren't there after the accident that took his sight. We went from a family to just the two of us in a heartbeat, and I promised myself I'd do everything in my power to take care of him. To give him the best life. Is my being with a wolf shifter living up to that promise?"

My stomach dropped and my heart nearly stopped. This had always been my fear, that telling her being my mate would affect Julian serving as the final nail in the coffin of our relationship.

Charlotte didn't give me a chance to respond. "How do we keep your secret from him if we all live together? What happens when he ages and I don't after you bite me?"

"How do you—"

She huffed. "I pay attention, you jerk. When you took me down to Chicago to meet those bosses of yours? That one supertall woman said she'd been mated to her husband for two hundred years, yet she didn't look a day over twenty-five. I know if we officially do the bite thing, my aging will slow to match yours." She grew quiet as her forehead landed on my chest. "Why didn't you tell me instead of making me figure it out?"

I sighed. I'd never voiced my worries to her or anyone else, not wanting to put that out into the universe and have it come true, but apparently it was time to address the elephant in the room. "I was afraid. I knew the difficulties of keeping the secret from Julian would be heavy for you, and I was too afraid you'd walk away from me instead of trying to find a solution."

She reared back, meeting my gaze. "Walk away? I love you, Abraham. Every single inch of my body craves you all the time. You've infiltrated my very soul; there's nowhere for me to go."

Even though I wanted to celebrate her words, they were delivered in such a way that I knew not to. "But?"

She seemed to shrink in on herself. "But…how do we deal with Julian? He's my brother, all I have left of my family. I won't turn my back on him or lie to him."

I shook my head as hope warmed my chest. This was a relatively easy problem to solve. It wasn't technically in line with NALB thinking, and I could get in trouble should anything go wrong, but the risk was infinitely worth the possible reward. "You don't have to."

"But the secret—"

I placed a finger against her lips and leaned close, fighting back my grin. "Fuck the secret. Julian's a good young man, one who means what he says and keeps his word. When he gets a little older, as long as we still feel we can trust him, we'll tell him. And we'll stress the importance of keeping it to himself. I don't doubt he will."

Charlotte's eyes grew hopeful. "We can tell him?"

"Yes, kitten. We can tell him. I trust him to understand that keeping the secret will keep all of us safe."

She wrapped her arms around my neck and pulled me close, her tears starting anew. "I thought that would be so much harder."

I shrugged, wanting to howl to the spirits that my greatest fear hadn't been realized. My mate was with me, and she might just want forever with me. "We'll work it out as time goes on. We'll figure it out. Because I love you and I don't want to give you up. Not for anything."

Charlotte leaned back, meeting my gaze once more. She stared for a long moment before saying, "I love you, Abraham Rebel Lynch. When I thought you'd died, it killed me. Gutted me completely. I don't want to go through that again."

"You won't."

"I don't want to lose you." Her tears fell once more, this time without the heart-wrenching sobs of earlier.

"You won't. I promise you." I pulled her in tight, rocking her again. "I've got you and Julian to take care of, my own little pack. Nothing's going to take me away from you."

Charlotte sniffed and took a deep breath. "Abraham?"

"Yeah, baby?" I kissed the top of her head, not willing to let her go just yet.

"I want us to exchange mating bites."

My world froze and then exploded in the colors of hope. I pulled back slowly, almost afraid to see her face. But when I did, her expression was clear and determined. "Are you—"

"Sure? I don't know. I'm still nervous about how this will affect Julian, and my heart gets ripped out of my chest every time I think about watching him die. But"—she looked up, fighting tears as she licked her bottom lip—"I watched you die tonight. I know now that it wasn't you, but in those few seconds when I thought it was, my entire world crashed. I don't want to do that again. I don't want to even consider the possibility of living without you. I'm yours and you're mine and we belong together. I want this…I want you."

Heart pounding in my chest and cock hardening almost against my will, I asked, "Forever?"

She nodded slowly as a smile crept across her face. "Forever."

I huffed and did my best to keep my hands from shaking. "When?"

She leaned forward, giving me a naughty smirk before she dropped her face to my neck. Licking a trail up my throat, making me groan as she rocked her hips against mine, she sighed.

"Now."

That was all I needed to hear. I pulled her close, my fingers sinking into the soft flesh of her ass as I kissed her with everything I had. I was more aggressive with her than normal, rocking her against my cock, rubbing myself against her clit. She moaned and made these breathy little huffs, a sign that she liked what I was doing. That it felt good. That I was on the right path.

Charlotte and I'd been together long enough for me to know most of what she liked. A little more pressure on her clit, a lot of growling when she was pressed against me, a little tease to her asshole. I did them all, making her huffs go to pants in mere minutes. But holding myself back just enough to keep her on edge.

"Rebel."

My name on her lips was an admonishment, but I didn't let up. I wanted her wet when I entered her, good and worked up when I finally gave in. And I wanted her completely focused on her orgasm when I bit her. While some shifters bit their mates often during sex, I doubted that would be something Charlotte enjoyed. If I was only getting the one chance, I was doing it right. For her. And for me.

I continued to rock her over my cock, feeling her slide easier with every pass. Teasing her with just enough of my cock to make her desperate and needy. She trembled in my arms, flushed and breathing hard. Close…already so close.

Sliding my hand around her thigh, I coated two fingers in her wetness, shivering as she groaned at the pressure.

"Rebel, please."

Growling my refusal, I squeezed her ass cheek harder with one hand as the other moved between the cheeks, wet fingers pressing on her asshole. Her groan was loud and deep, making me growl in response to her obvious arousal. Fuck, this woman was so sexy. So ridiculously beautiful. I could play with her like this all day and never grow tired of it.

Carefully, gently, I nudged one wet finger in her ass, loving the way Charlotte shivered and gasped at the intrusion. Meanwhile, I kept pulling her over my cock, not entering, but teasing her clit with every pass.

"Rebel."

This time my name came out with a bit of frustration tingeing the words. I understood that. My cock was rock hard and ready to be buried inside her warmth. The heat and wet rubbing against my skin were making it hard to keep from angling just a bit, sliding inside, but I wanted a little more. I needed to hear her begging for my cock.

After pumping in and out a few times, I slid a second finger into her ass. Charlotte made a sound halfway between a groan and a scream as she dropped her head back. I took the opportunity to lean down and bite one perfectly hard nipple, pulling it into my mouth, suckling.

"Fuck, please, Rebel. Need you."

I gave her nipple one final pull then popped off, still working my fingers in and out of her ass. "You ready for my cock, kitten? Are you good and wet for me?"

"Fuck…yes. Want you now. I'm ready."

I pulled her in for a deep kiss as I shifted her hips a bit, lining myself up. "Is this what you want?"

She nodded, refastening our lips and stroking her tongue inside my mouth. With a groan, I pulled her onto my cock. She slid down slowly, letting me go deep in a single press. The heat and pressure of her surrounding me made me shiver as my thigh and core muscles clenched. Fuck, the woman was so tight.

Charlotte lifted herself and sank down again, riding me, taking what she needed. I sat back and let her, keeping my fingers flexing in her ass, helping her build toward that pleasure precipice. She felt so good, her walls holding my cock in a warm, wet vise. Too good. I wanted to come so badly, my balls were starting to ache, but I knew she had to go first. Tonight was about us, coming together as mates, bonding in the final way we needed to reach our forever. My own pleasure could take a back seat.

"Gonna…oh God, gonna come. Rebel, gonna…"

"Go, kitten. I've got you." I spread my fingers inside her, stretching her tight ring a little more. She shivered and groaned and lost her rhythm, speeding up as her walls fluttered around me. Cursing, biting her lip, fucking me into the floor.

And when she came, when her body clamped down on my cock in a death grip the likes of which I'd never experienced, I yanked her upper body to me and sank my teeth into the flesh of her breast. She clawed her nails down my back, chanting my name, shaking and trembling and riding me through her orgasm.

My balls pulled up tight to my body, my need to come almost painful, but I couldn't. Not yet. Not until I made sure I'd claimed her completely. I sucked and licked her breast, feeling the presence of her grow inside me. I kept at it until she slumped against my shoulder, sated. Removing my fingers carefully, I let go of her breast and lapped at the wound.

"My kitten," I whispered, growling my words. "So fucking amazing."

She moaned and rocked just a bit. "Your turn, Rebel."

I hummed in response, too turned on to speak. But it was more than just lust. I wanted her bite. I wanted her to claim me. Wanted it as I'd never wanted anything so much in my very long life. I'd died my human death and become a shifter fighting for a freedom I felt I couldn't live without. But I knew, I'd learned, my freedom had been a myth. I hadn't found true freedom until I'd been tied to this amazing, beautiful, wonderful woman. And I wanted that forever.

Charlotte pulled back, rotating her hips as she angled herself over me. "Here?" she asked as she fingered my pec.

I swallowed hard, barely paying attention as she rode my cock. "Wherever you want."

She peered at me from heavy-lidded eyes, watching, inspecting. "Anywhere?"

"Of course."

She smirked, her fingers trailing over my nipples and down my chest. "Where do most women…do it?"

I huffed a laugh, gripping her hips and moving her over me. Desperate to come but even more desperate for her to pick a fucking spot and get on with it. I couldn't wait any longer to know I was hers. "The neck, the chest, I've heard of men with claiming bites on their ass or thighs."

"I'm so not biting your ass."

I leaned forward, stealing a sloppy kiss. "You love my ass."

She hummed. "I do, but I'm not biting it."

"Too bad."

She suddenly looked nervous. "I'm not doing this right, am I?"

"What are you talking about?" I asked as fear slid down my spine.

"I should have bitten you when you bit me, right? Like, it would have meant more or something?"

"Charlotte, no." I wrapped my arms around her, holding her close. "Some mates don't even exchange bites on the same day. One goes first, but the other waits. And some couples exchange bites within minutes of meeting. Every couple's different. You're not messing up anything."

She stopped rocking, her eyes meeting mine as she chewed on her lip. "I don't want to hurt you."

I shook my head. "You won't."

"But I have to draw blood." Her whispered words practically made me smile. She was worried about a little blood?

"You already did." I motioned over my shoulder. She leaned forward, her hair tickling my face as she looked down my back.

"Oh, holy fuck." She moved back, her eyes wide. "I can't believe I did that."

"Again. You did it again." I grinned as she gave me an apologetic frown. "A little bite is nothing compared to claw marks. And I've been sporting those for months."

She flinched and scrunched her nose. "I'm sorry."

"I'm not." I kissed that squished-up nose. Adorable. "I love that you were so turned on. I wear those marks with pride."

Her shoulders eased and a smile began to creep across her

face. "And my bite?"

"Same thing. I'll show that off to anyone who comes near. It's a sign of pride. A sign that someone viewed me good enough to claim as their own, forever. There's no greater honor."

Charlotte smirked and resumed moving her hips, sliding me in and out a little on each pass. "So you want me to bite you where people can see it?"

My growl came out without my intention. "Wherever you want."

Charlotte smirked, seeing right through me. Fuck, of course I wanted her to bite me where others could see it. I'd waited centuries to meet my mate. I wanted the whole fucking world to know I'd found her.

Hips moving faster and harder, she leaned toward me, nibbling and licking along my collarbone. I met her thrusts, dropping my head back and giving in as she tormented my flesh with her mouth. Every touch made me jump; every pause had my gut clenching as I wondered if that was it, if she'd bite into me in the next moment.

"Rebel?"

I groaned, loving the way her whisper cooled my overheated skin. "Yeah, kitten?"

"I love you."

Before I could answer, she bit down on my neck, sinking her teeth deep in my flesh. I clutched her to me, my hips pumping of their own volition as I came inside her. The pain of it all making everything sharper and more intense. I cradled the back of her head, wanting the moment to last. The burn of her bite, the softness of her body against mine, the way her pussy cradled my cock. A moment of pure perfection, and it was all ours.

When I finally took a deep breath and eased my hold on her, nearly spent, Charlotte pulled her mouth from my neck. Not ready to let her go, I grabbed her face and pulled her to me for a deep kiss. My tongue tangled with hers as my heartbeat slowed to a normal pace, giving me time to think about what I needed to say to her.

I broke the kiss, rested my forehead against hers, and whispered the words I'd waited two centuries to say. "You are my mate, my everything. I honor that bond and will do everything to keep it strong. You're my world, Charlotte Andrews, and I will love you until the end of time."

She smiled, all flushed and glowing in the moonlight streaming through the windows. "Back atcha, handsome."

We snuggled for a few moments, being silly and grinning like lunatics, before she finally sighed said, "So…we're bonded to each other forever?"

I raised an eyebrow, knowing she was going somewhere with that question. "Yeah?"

She nodded once, bit her lip, and then shrugged. "What's next?"

"Well, first, I go wash my hands," I said with a chuckle, loving as her face flushed in embarrassment. "And then… whatever we want. It doesn't matter what we do next as long as we do it together. With Julian."

Her grin twisted up as if she'd just bitten into a lemon. "Please don't mention my little brother when I'm straddling you…naked."

I laughed and yanked her closer. "Yeah, sorry. I won't do that again."

She shook her head against my chest as she giggled. "Never."

Pulling her back so I could look her in the eye, I grinned and winked. "Never again. Not a single day of our forever."

DEATH OF A WITCH

Phoenix & Azurine

November: Takes Place Shortly After *Claiming His Witch*

Phoenix

My leg bounced as I watched Zuri try again and again to fasten a necklace. I'd asked to help her, but she'd turned me down. Vehemently. It was a gift to her from Sarah, she'd said. Some kind of magickal talisman or totem, and she could put it on herself. Or so she claimed. She'd tried numerous times already but hadn't been able to link the ends together. So I sat, and I waited, and I watched the woman who'd completely claimed my heart fight back tears as she struggled with a thin chain of gold.

Sarah was ready to leave for the Summerlands.

I had no idea how she knew it was her time to die, but the old witch was adamant. One more day and then she would be leaving our realm for another. But first, she wanted us to say our goodbyes.

Zuri and I had barely slept after receiving the call from Sarah's niece the night before. Instead, we'd spent the darkest hours of the night wrapped up in each other and ignoring everything that existed outside the four walls of the cabin. But it was morning, and the world couldn't be ignored another moment. It was time for Amber, Scarlett, and my mate to say goodbye to the woman who'd raised them.

I bit my thumbnail as I watched Zuri huff and drop her arms, the jewelry still not hanging around her neck. Her hands shook as she refocused on the mirror, raising the fine threads of gold and dipping her head to reach behind herself. The gold vibrated against her chest in a way that told me she'd fail again. But I sat…and I bounced my knee…and I waited.

Until the first tear fell.

I was up and crowding her deeper into the bathroom in a heartbeat, my stomach against her back, a low growl rumbling in my chest.

"Please." I ran my fingers down her arms, from elbows to wrists, giving her a chance to refuse me once again. But I needed to help her. I couldn't stand to see her struggle, even with something as trivial as putting on a necklace. We both knew her problems with the clasp had nothing to do with the jewelry itself; they were deeply rooted in the meaning behind the piece. The symbolism the necklace held.

"I can do it." She sniffed and moved to pull away, but I wrapped my fingers around her wrists and held her in place.

"Please."

Her eyes met mine in the mirror as my whispered plea seemed to finally register. Bloodshot, sea-green eyes looked back at me. My heart broke at the expression on her face. The endless pain on display.

I nudged closer, leaning in until my lips were mere millimeters from hers. "Let me help you."

She held my gaze for a moment before handing the necklace to me. "Okay."

I fumbled a bit with the thin chain, my big hands unaccustomed to something so fine and delicate. But after a few seconds, I hooked one side through the other and settled the metal against her skin. She adjusted the oval stone hanging from the chain to rest right at the top of her cleavage and gave me the saddest little smile ever.

"Thanks."

"Anytime." I rested my hands on her shoulders and breathed her in. "You look beautiful."

She snorted a laugh. "No, I don't, but thanks for trying."

I pressed a kiss to her cheek, her jaw, her ear. "You're always beautiful," I whispered.

She peered at me in the mirror, her eyes reflecting a sadness I ached to fix. But there was no fixing this. There was only supporting her, loving her, and making sure I was there to catch her when she fell. Because she would fall. I knew it without her having to say a word. She loved Sarah like a mother, and losing her would be heartbreaking. Even as hard as she was fighting and as strong as I knew her to be, the grief would pull her under.

But not quite yet.

"We should probably start packing for Detroit soon." Zuri looked away and tried to smile, but it fell flat. The move to the other side of the state was another topic we'd been avoiding. And one Zuri apparently thought would work as a distraction from the death of her friend and mentor.

I shook my head, not willing to let her hide from the reality of the day. "Not yet. Not until you're ready."

"With Sarah gone, there's no point—"

"Not until you're ready." I crouched down and turned her around to face me. "We're staying right here in this cabin until you and your sisters are ready to move. Detroit can wait."

"But your job…"

I sighed and pulled her into my arms. "My mate comes before my job. Always."

She clung to me, her hands shaking as they fisted the back of my sweater. Fuck, I wanted to wrap her up and take her to bed with me. I wanted to make a nest out of the covers and just…be. Let her deal with all the shit in her head while I kept the rest of the world at bay. But that was not in the cards for us.

A soft knock at the door was the only warning before Beast appeared in the cabin. "Time to go."

With a sigh and one last squeeze, Zuri dropped her forehead to my chest. "I hate this." Her voice was a whisper, a breath of pain and heartache.

"I know, baby." I closed my eyes and held her tight, wishing I could give her my strength for the next few hours.

Eventually, I directed Zuri outside, keeping my hands on her the whole way. The sky was dark for the time of day. Dappled gray clouds blocked the sun and kept a slight fog hovering over the snow-covered ground. And while the gloom could've been attributed to the fact that it was December in Michigan, I had a feeling it was more Zuri's doing. Her emotional climate. The magick within her affecting the weather once again.

The trek through the woods seemed to take no time at all, and soon enough we made the final curve to see the old lighthouse standing tall and proud at the inlet to Lake Parity. Amber and Scarlett stood on the front porch holding hands, looking small and so very young all of a sudden. Zuri rushed to them, the three embracing in a way that made my soul ache. There was a desperation in the way they clutched each other, a need to support each other even though each one was falling apart.

"Ready?" Scarlett whispered to Zuri as Beast and I reached the girls. The three pulled apart, all with matching red-rimmed eyes and sad expressions. I wrapped an arm around Zuri, pulling her against me.

"I know this is hard on you," I whispered into her hair. She nodded and her breath caught as she fought back tears.

With my arm still wrapped around my mate, I turned to direct Amber and Scarlett to the front door. The two girls took a synchronized breath and grasped hands, a unit of two. Scarlett reached her free hand toward me, looking up into my eyes with an expression filled with fear. I clasped her hand in mine and pulled her tight to my side, still holding Zuri, Amber clinging to Scarlett's hand.

Weavers are never singular entities, Adam. We are linked—tied together through the thread of life.

I nearly shook my head as Ximena's voice floated through my mind. A reminder of when I'd met the mother of the Weaver triplets in the Summerlands. Of the time I'd technically been dead. These women were my responsibility, and all three of them were suffering through losing the only parent they'd ever known. Yet I had no clue how to help them.

We followed Amber into the lighthouse, Zuri moving to grip Scarlett's hand. I lagged behind, watchful and protective but out of the way. Beast would guard the house from outdoors. This was a private moment, one for Zuri and her sisters, and I could respect that. But I couldn't leave my mate's side. Not when I knew she would need me.

When we reached the front staircase, Zuri froze, her eyes drawn to a room draped in white fabric and glowing with the light from hundreds of black candles. It would have been beautiful if not for how stark it seemed. Glancing back at Zuri, pain lanced across my heart. Her face was pale, her eyes wide and brimming with tears as she looked into that room. What she knew versus what I saw had to be two different things. She'd said the color of the candles burning had significance, but I didn't know what black meant.

"She's not dead yet."

Amber turned at Zuri's whisper, her eyes wide. "Pardon?"

Zuri pointed to the room. "Why is the room prepared if Sarah's not dead yet?"

"Because she's dying." Amber stood, hands clasped in front of her, her expression sad and regretful.

Zuri faltered under the gaze of her sister. "I just didn't think—"

"I know." Amber reached for Zuri's hand and gave her younger sister a small smile. "Sarah's ready to go; setting the parlor up for her funeral was what she wanted me to do. So I didn't have to worry about it after. I never meant to upset you."

Zuri looked into the room again, pursing her lips. Slowly, she squared her shoulders and took a deep breath. "Yeah, okay. I can see that. I'm sorry I wasn't here to help you. I should have been. We could have come—"

Amber shook her head. "Stop. It's fine. It gave me something to do while the rest of the coven said their goodbyes."

"Yeah, and asked her for all her magickal tips and tricks," Scarlett scoffed from the bottom of the stairs. "I swear, death brings out the worst in people."

Amber sighed and closed her eyes for a moment. "It's been hard on all of us. Some just don't handle the loss as well as others."

I followed the girls up the stairs, noting as always how pale the house was. Whitewashed floors, white walls, and white fixtures. It was as if someone had tossed a gallon of milk in the house as a decorating style. Zuri was always telling me how warm our cabin was, how inviting. I could understand why she felt that way. This place was a house of ice.

We moved as a unit down a long hallway to a pair of whitewashed wooden doors with glass handles. Even the hinges were painted white. The lack of color made my wolf instincts surge. Though, to be honest, I'd been fighting a shift since the moment we stepped outside of our little cabin in the woods. Everything about this day was making my wolf anxious.

"She's tired and weak," Amber said as we reached the door to Sarah's room. "But she's really looking forward to all of us being here." She moved to open the door but then caught me staring at her and smiled. "Especially you."

I grinned and ducked my head. "We get along well."

Scarlett snorted a laugh. "Please. The lady thinks you're hot and is jealous of all the action Zuri's getting. If it wasn't so hilarious to see you blushing and stuttering as she flirts with you, it'd be disgusting."

Zuri's face grew red. "You guys, she's an old lady."

"So?" Scarlett shrugged. "She's not dead yet."

Amber groaned. "I can't believe you just said that."

Scarlet rolled her eyes as Zuri chuckled. "What? It's true."

"That doesn't make it right," Amber said. "For the love of—"

"Hot damn, children. Can't an old woman die in peace around here?"

The girls all turned toward the doors, which were no longer closed. Sarah leaned against the jamb, her weathered hands clutching the edges of her robe.

"Sarah, you should be resting." Amber moved to grab Sarah's arm, but the older woman waved her off.

"And I would be if you girls hadn't been out here making so much racket." She glanced over our group, her eyes lighting on each woman in turn before stopping at me. "Hello, Adam."

I nodded once. "Good morning, ma'am."

She scowled. "Cut the ma'am crap; you make me feel old. Girls, quit trying to embarrass this handsome young man. I'd be mad if he stopped his daily visits."

"Never." I gave her my biggest smile.

She snorted. "Yes, well, once I'm in the Summerlands, they'll end. You can't exactly come visit me when I'm dead, now can you?"

She glanced back at me, an impish glint in her eyes. As I'd spent time with her these past few weeks, she'd occasionally made offhand comments that had me wondering if she knew something. Something about what happened to me when I died. But she'd never been direct. That question of hers combined with her knowing look was the closest she'd come to telling me she knew my secret.

Sarah settled herself in her bed with the help of Zuri, watching my girl the whole time. "I didn't see it before, but I do now."

Zuri smiled even as her eyebrows drew together, "See what?"

"Your bond to him. You told me he was your red thread, but I couldn't see." She tapped her temple before leaning back against her pillows. "I see it now. The glow tying you to him. It's love's radiance, isn't it? The other half to your soul."

Zuri glanced up at me, her cheeks growing dark. I gave her a smile. Our love was something private between us, but it wasn't something we hid. If Sarah could see it, then she could see *us*. The true us. Our bond to one another.

Sarah chuckled as she watched Zuri blush and hurry to straighten the bedding. I wanted to relax, but the scent of death and rot teased me. Subtle, not yet permeating the air. But even the hint of it made the hair on the back of my neck stand up. The woman didn't have long for this world. And by the way she stared at the girls, drinking in every detail, I knew she'd miss them.

As if I'd called to her with my thoughts, she glanced my way. Her watery eyes met mine, and she gave a small nod of her head. "Thank you for keeping Zuri safe."

I gave a subtle bow. "It's my pleasure."

Her voice lowered, her face turning serious. "Thank you for keeping them all…balanced."

I froze, remembering Ximena's words from the Summerlands.

Magick must have balance. It must be equal on all sides. Azurine and Scarlett are balanced against each other. Fire and water, opposite powers that keep the other in check. But my Amber…

The old woman said nothing else, at least not to me. Sarah and the girls talked for almost two hours after that. Reminiscing. Saying their goodbyes as they celebrated their pasts. It was beautiful to watch. I sat in a small armchair in the corner, completely out of the way and apparently forgotten by the women in the room. Two hours of laughter and tears, stories, and secrets. I learned a lot about the four of them as I sat in that uncomfortable chair.

Like the fact that Scarlett had a huge bark but very little bite and would back down immediately with just a glance from Sarah. Like that Amber was the serious one of the group, but she also had a sarcastic sense of humor that kept me chuckling. And Zuri, my beautiful Zuri, was the heart between them, always smiling and offering sweet words to make the others smile as well.

When Sarah began coughing, the force of it causing her to curl in on herself, all three girls jumped to help her.

"I'll go get some tea." Amber moved toward the door, but Sarah stopped her with a gasp.

"No, I need you." She glanced between the girls, waving her hand. "Let Azurine get it. I want a moment with you."

With a quick look in my direction, Zuri left the room. After three seconds of her being out of my sight, the anxiousness building in my gut got to me. I moved to stand, to follow my mate, but Sarah waved me down.

"You stay put." She glanced over at Scarlett. "But you need to go. I have a few things that only the Phoenix and Amber should hear."

The anxiety I'd felt all day grew. She'd said my road name. She'd never called me anything but Adam since Zuri first brought me to meet her.

"Don't look so surprised." Sarah adjusted herself in her bed, obviously in pain, as Scarlett walked out and closed the door. "I've been dancing in and out of the Summerlands for a week now. You're quite the hero over there."

"You were in the Summerlands?" Amber asked, looking at me with surprise. Her expression transformed into one of near-horror when I shrugged. "Oh, when I—"

"Enough, you two." Sarah tried to sound stern, but there was a weakness to her voice that she couldn't disguise. "We have much to talk about before Azurine gets back."

"Yes, ma'am." Amber nodded, looking sad and guilty. I hated seeing her that way, knowing she was probably beating herself up over our…introduction. Killing your sister's soul mate and sending them to the witch version of the afterlife wasn't exactly the best how-do-you-do.

"Hey." I caught her eye as she looked up. "I forgave you that day. It was an honest mistake. You thought you were helping Rebel, and I've got nothing but respect for that. There's no blame coming from me."

"But"—she swallowed and looked away—"I killed you."

I nearly shivered as the reality of her words flowed over me. "Yeah, well, I made it back, so…" I shrugged, swallowing down the anger and distrust I tried not to feel around her. "We're cool."

She paused, wide eyes staring at me as if I was insane. And maybe I was. The witch had collapsed my lungs and suffocated me with her magick. I probably should have wanted to rip her throat out for that, but she was Zuri's sister. I couldn't hate my mate's sibling; it would just hurt Zuri in the end.

"You two are so good together," Sarah said as she beamed at Amber. "Your mother chose well."

Amber shook her head. "I'm not his soul mate."

"No, you're not." Sarah sat up a bit more. "But you're joined to him."

Amber looked concerned. "Joined? Like how?"

"Like how you've become bonded to your elemental balancer."

The two of them looked at me, staring, making me feel like a specimen under a microscope. "What?"

"Come here, young man." Sarah waved me over. "I've only

just been told about this, and I need you closer to be sure."

I approached the bed, giving Sarah my hand when she held out hers. She stared into my eyes for many seconds, mumbling words that sounded to be in another language. And then she smiled.

"Yes. Yes, finally."

I glanced from her to Amber and back. "Finally what?"

"A spirit to balance the elements." Sarah smiled in a self-satisfied way as my eyebrows drew together and Amber looked on in what could only be described as fearful shock.

"I…have no idea what you're talking about."

"Really?" Sarah choked on a laugh, coughing for a few moments before finally catching her breath once more. "So you didn't make a pledge to Ximena while in the Summerlands? You didn't promise to be the triplets' balance?"

My heart nearly stopped, and I coughed to clear my throat. "Well—"

"You spoke to our mom?" Amber looked at me with a mix of excitement and hurt on her face, making me feel about six inches tall.

"Hold on, Amber. I want to make sure we all know everything before we move on." Sarah gave me a solid once-over, almost a Rebel-worthy inspection before leaning closer, her eyes bright and her skin flushed. "The Weavers practice elemental magick—the ingrained powers of the air, water, fire, and earth. I assume you realize Scarlett is a fire witch."

I shrugged. "I've seen her go sparky a time or two."

"That's one way to describe it. Remind her to tell you about the year she set my porch on fire. I could still wring her neck for that one." Sarah settled against her pillows once more. "Azurine is a water witch, also known as a siren in certain cultures. Don't let her sing near the water; you'll drown yourself in your lust for her."

I coughed and glanced down at my feet for a second. "Oh…

okay."

Amber rolled her eyes. "Really, Sarah? Pulling out the siren legends for Zuri? I thought we were past all that."

Sarah waved her hand and scoffed at the younger witch. "Sirens are the succubae of the witch world, embracing their sexuality in an almost obsessive fashion. Good for you on land, young Adam. Not so much in the water."

"Jesus," I whispered as my face burned. I was not prepared to talk about Zuri's sexuality with the woman who'd raised her. That was just…too much, no matter what the situation was.

"Don't be a prude." Sarah tossed a wadded-up tissue at me. "So Azurine and Scarlett are a matched set; their elements balance when they work in tandem. And balance to an elemental witch is everything."

I huffed, still uncomfortable and embarrassed. "I may have heard that before."

"I bet you have." Sarah nodded and smiled. "When a witch primarily focuses her craft on elemental magick, she needs an opposite element to balance out the power. Fire and water; air and earth. But Amber has always been the lone air witch of her generation, with no earth witch to create that sense of balance. Her magick is not as strong as the witches who find their opposite element, yet it tends to overtake her in times of stress. That's why her mother made sure to bring the girls here, to me. I'm a strong enough earth witch for her to rely on, and I've spent the last twenty-plus years being the balance for Amber."

Sarah smirked, looking so damned proud of herself. "But not any longer. And this is where you tell us about meeting Ximena."

My stomach dropped as I shook my head. "I…can't. I don't know why, but it doesn't feel right."

"But you spoke to her—my mother?" Amber's face fell as Sarah frowned.

I nodded. "Yes. She's the reason I was able to come back."

Amber nodded, looking a little sad. "So what does this have to do with my magick? He's not a witch."

Sarah shook her head. "No, but he carries the wolf within. The spirit animal of the earth witch. The Fates may have pulled him to Azurine as a mate, but they also pulled him to *you* in an effort to save you before that magickal imbalance cost you."

"Cost her what?" I glanced from one woman to the other, waiting for an answer.

Finally, Sarah said, "Unbalanced witches tend to fall victim to dark forces. The power of a single element is too strong without the second person absorbing some of the energy. Without an earth witch to balance you, Amber, you could turn to the darker sides of magick. You already were."

The two shared a long look, one filled with a meaning I was missing.

"What do you mean, she already was?" I asked.

Amber shook her head and turned her back to me as Sarah sighed.

"She lost a piece of herself there for a bit." Sarah held up a hand as I went to speak, her eyes focusing on Amber. I watched as the younger witch's shoulders shook.

"I didn't think you knew." Amber's harsh whisper was filled with pain.

"I raised you, loved you like one of my own. Of course I knew." Sarah's voice was quiet but strong, filled with emotions I couldn't have named. "I knew the moment my magick began to weaken that you were in danger. It's why I kept trying to call to your mother. Why I cast every spell in the grimoire that had to do with the Summerlands. I knew Ximena would see how to help you; I just had to find a way to reach her."

"I didn't want to disappoint you," Amber murmured.

"I know, but you put your sisters at risk by not telling them that you were struggling. And you hurt Azurine horribly when you agreed to kick her out of the coven. That was when I knew

I needed to try one last time to reach Ximena. You were losing control, causing your sister so much pain, and I couldn't allow that."

"I felt so out of control. And the smell of him on her…" Amber shook her head.

Sarah sighed and met my eyes. "We don't believe in the devil or evil per se, but the dark forces of magick can be very compelling. When I first grew ill, Amber struggled to find her balance between the dark and the light side of magick. And the worse I felt, the harder it was for her. That hatred she felt before she even met you was the darkness trying to keep her away from the one thing that could bring her back to rights. She pushed Zuri away to keep you from getting close to her. She killed you because of it."

Fury slammed into my gut. I growled as Amber turned, the two of us staring at each other. "But you and Ximena think I can balance her."

"Yes. I do believe you're the key to keeping her on the light side of the magickal realm."

I nodded, trying to ease back the urge to shift and attack as the memories of Zuri—wet and cold and running away from this very house—brought back my rage. Damn it…Amber had hurt my mate. Had been the cause of so much pain to the woman I loved. No matter how much forgiveness I threw around, that was a hard pill to swallow.

I glanced at the offending witch, collecting my thoughts and searching for words when all I wanted to do was bark and growl.

"I've already forgiven you for the spell you cast on me," I finally said as I stepped toward Amber. "I won't go back on that. But you hurt Zuri, and that's a lot harder for me to brush off. She's my mate, my soul, the most important thing in my life." I crowded the witch, walked right into her personal space, forcing her to look up into my eyes. "If you ever feel out of balance again, you tell me. If you ever think these dark spirits are closing in, you tell me. If you feel even a touch more blue than normal, you tell me. Because if you hurt Zuri again, if anything you do threatens her in any way, I won't be so forgiving."

Amber swallowed hard as she stared at me, only breaking eye contact to nod. "I can control it."

I glanced at Sarah, unsure if I should believe her. "You'd better."

Sarah gave me a small smile, her skin pale and her breathing labored. "Zuri and Amber are a part of one another, along with Scarlett. Sisters, born of the same womb. Conceived on the summer solstice by an elemental witch and a man with the power of divination. These girls are powerful, bred of magick and intuition. But they've never had an earth witch to ground them in the present. As much as I tried, my magick was too old to truly bond with them. That's your job."

I huffed, still fighting back a snarl. "I don't know how to be her balance."

"Yes, you do." Sarah coughed again, her face growing pale. "Deep down, you know exactly what to do. Your energy is already working on Amber, and I see the thread between the sisters drawing tighter every day."

Sarah pulled me closer, the paper-thin skin on her hands growing white around the knuckles as she gripped my shirt. "You will love Azurine in a way that no witch has experienced in generations. And she'll love you just as deeply. But as Ximena said, she's a package deal. She cannot truly be happy without the grounding her opposite element gives her, and the same goes for Scarlett. Amber has never found the peace that comes from that balance, and therefore has never had as close of a bond with her sisters as she should have. The other earth witches of the coven have tried to help her, but her power is too unstable. Too hard to contain. She needs someone with an inner strength and a will that rivals her own."

"But what does that mean?" I asked. "What do I do?"

Sarah smiled as she fell back against the pillows. "It means love your Azurine. Take care of her. Make many more babies with her. But pay attention to Amber. Care for her as a brother would. She's going to need you."

I swallowed hard, whispering my greatest fear. "Will she hurt Zuri?"

Sarah shook her head. "No, dear. Amber loves her sister. With you by her side, she'll stay on the path of the light."

She closed her eyes as Zuri walked in followed by a curious-looking Scarlett.

"Everything okay in here?" Scarlett asked.

I stared at Amber, both of us silent. For everything that she'd done to me, I could forgive her. Easily. But all I could remember at that moment was the look on Zuri's face when she came running into camp after she was banished from the coven. The pain and anguish she felt. And I grew angry once more.

But then I remembered my time in the Summerlands with Ximena. The three little girls. Scarlett and Azurine had played so well together, but Amber had walked away. Not left out, but not fitting in. I knew that feeling. I could understand it as only someone who never really fit in could. After my parents kicked me out, I'd been the kid without a place to belong. I still felt that way at times.

I walked over to Amber, wishing for the strength I needed to say the words I knew had to be said. For a few long moments, we just stood in front of one another, staring as if waiting for the other to balk.

"I'm good if you are." It was the closest I could come to acceptance. She'd have to earn more from me, not by the way she treated me, but by the way she treated my Zuri.

Amber smiled, slow and soft, looking so much like Ximena in that moment, she nearly stole my breath. "I'm fine."

My girls all need you in their life, young one: Zuri as her lover and soul mate, Scarlett as her friend, and Amber as the person to keep her balanced and connected to the world. Without you, each will fall. Starting with Amber.

Sighing, feeling Ximena's spirit nearby as I surrendered to my chosen fate, I pulled Amber into a loose hug. "I've got you, sis."

Amber took a deep, shuddering breath. "I'm so sorry for all of it. I never meant—"

"Oh, no." The sound of my mate's distress had me spinning before Amber could finish her sentence. My heart broke as I saw the devastated looks on Zuri's and Scarlett's faces, and I wrapped an arm around Amber as she gasped. The three girls and I stepped forward, approaching the bed as their tears began to fall. Sarah lay still and peaceful, her hand hanging off the edge of the mattress. There was no more heartbeat, no more rattled breathing.

Sarah, former high priestess of the Lake Parity coven and only mother my mate had ever known, had passed on.

Take care of my babies.

I pulled the three girls together, creating my very own family of four as we mourned the passing of a friend, the end of an era.

As we grieved for the death of a witch.

THE CAR REVEALED

Phoenix & Azurine

December: Takes Place Shortly After *Death of a Witch*

Phoenix

"Someday, boy," Beast said as he tightened the final strap across the bed of his truck, "you're going to quit thanking me."

I shrugged. "I'll quit thanking you the day you stop doing so much for me."

Beast stared at me, those blue eyes of his filled with an emotion I knew he'd never be able to put into words. But I felt it. I knew it. He was family in ways no one else would ever be. He'd saved my life twice, and he was giving up a lot to make the move to Detroit with the girls and me.

After a long moment, Beast took a deep breath and clasped my shoulder.

"You're my blood. *Mi hermano.* There's nothing I wouldn't do for you." He pushed me back, releasing my shoulder as he snorted a laugh. "So quit thanking me all the goddamned time."

I grinned as he gave me a one-sided smile. "All right, old man. Though we'll see if you're so gracious once you get Amber and Scarlett under your roof."

All three Weaver sisters walked out of the lighthouse at that moment. They looked tired and worn down. The weeks since Sarah passed had taken a toll on them, but they were smiling.

Each one ready for their new adventure.

"I still can't believe you're taking on triplets." Beast leaned against the bed of his truck, which was filled with boxes of belongings from the Weaver girls. It was moving day, and all five of us were heading to Detroit. Amber and Scarlett would move in with Beast, as he had more space at the townhouse he kept there than I did. Zuri would come with me to my little apartment on the north side of the city. A tiny, shabby den for just the two of us. I couldn't wait.

Thinking of my mate moving into my home made me smile. "They're a package deal."

Beast huffed, looking completely unconvinced. "Any luck on finding a new place?"

I grinned as Zuri met my gaze from across the snow-covered lawn, her own smile growing to match mine. "I have a few options. The Realtor said things would open up a bit more in January, but I'm not sure I want to wait. The girls need each other."

The women in question approached, all three wearing long skirts and heavy coats. Snow covered the ground, drifting knee-high in places. Beast and I'd cleared the walkway earlier so the coven wouldn't be hampered in whatever they needed to do, but more snow was coming, and I was worried. With the Weaver sisters leaving, the chores would only get harder for the aging coven. But we were cutting ties with the women who'd banished my mate, which meant there was nothing more I could do for them.

I welcomed Zuri into my arms, snuggling her against my body and relishing the heat she gave off. "You girls about ready to go?"

"Ready as we'll ever be." Amber looked back at the lighthouse, squinting. "It's still fuzzy. I can't see past the blur."

Zuri turned her head toward her sister. "Maybe because we're leaving. You can't see anything regarding the future of the lighthouse because you won't be here."

"Maybe." Amber didn't sound convinced.

"C'mon, you slowpokes. Let's get this caravan started." Scarlett pulled open the door of Beast's truck and grinned. "I think the three of us should skedaddle before the young one over there sees Zuri's car. I, for one, have no interest in seeing him cream his jeans."

Zuri shook against my chest, laughing. Both her sisters quickly joined in while Beast looked about as confused as I felt.

"What the hell do you drive, girl?"

"You'll see," Scarlett singsonged. She pulled herself up into the truck, followed closely by Amber. Just before they slammed the passenger door closed, Scarlett turned the volume on the radio up. An old Madonna song came screaming from the vehicle. Beast growled as the truck began to rock from Scarlett's manic seat-dancing.

"Could be worse." I shrugged as Beast spun in my direction. "She could've picked show tunes."

His growl deepened as he glared. "Well, this'll be a fun four hours." Beast stalked toward the driver's side door as Zuri and I laughed.

"She's going to torture him." Zuri leaned back to meet my gaze, a true smile on her beautiful face.

"Yeah, she totally is."

We watched as the truck drove off before heading toward the old barn that served as a garage for the coven.

"So," I said as we reached the concrete apron. "I finally get to see this supersecret car of yours."

"Yep. My baby and I have been together for six years now. I usually try not to take her out too much in the winter, but I can't stand the thought of leaving her behind."

I followed Zuri into the barn, which was lined on one side with the cars owned by the coven. Lots of tan and silver sedans, a minivan, even a small pickup truck. None of them looked like something my Zuri would drive, though. And I was right. She walked right past the cars to a spot in the back corner where a silver tarp covered what was undoubtedly a car.

"You ready for this?" Zuri gave me a smirk over her shoulder and leaned down to grab the edge of the tarp. I swallowed hard as her coat rode up, exposing the curve of her ass. Even covered from head to toe as she was, the woman had a sexy silhouette. That ass, that bent-over pose—damn, she made me want to mount her from behind and fuck her until we couldn't stand any longer.

I crossed my arms over my chest and tried to stop thinking about how hot and soft she'd be wrapped around my dick. "Give it to me."

I wanted her to give it to me all right, but that desire had nothing to do with a car. The past few weeks had been exhausting for Zuri. From the funeral to packing up Sarah's belongings, Zuri's emotions had been put through the wringer, which meant we'd been doing little more than sharing a bed at night. Not that I minded, but she was the most arousing woman I'd ever seen, even when not trying to be—especially when not trying to be—which meant I was rocking a set of blue balls like never before.

I wanted her. I craved her. I needed her, and hopefully soon, I'd have her again. Once she was ready. I wouldn't pressure her. God knew, the woman was worth the wait.

With a smile and a wink, Zuri yanked the tarp into the aisle. All thoughts of sex left my mind as the delicious curves of classic American muscle filled my senses.

"Holy shit, Camaro." My whisper came out prayerlike in the quiet space.

"Nineteen sixty-nine Yenko Camaro, to be exact." The smugness in Zuri's voice matched the lustful gleam in her eye as she walked the tarp backward to expose the rear end of what could only be called a masterpiece of metal. "Four-twenty-seven engine, power disc brakes, and an M-21 four-speed trans. Only about two hundred Yenkos were made that year."

"Two hundred and one," I whispered, still staring at the black beast. The front spoiler screamed aggression, the cowl-induction hood sitting menacingly beneath the windshield. This car was meant for speed, for racing. For everything fast and loud. I swallowed hard, itching to drive the beauty but too afraid Zuri would turn me down to ask. "The color's not right."

Zuri laughed. "Original owner had it painted tuxedo black. Otherwise"—she walked the length of the car, running a finger along the topline in a way that made me whimper—"it's cherry."

"Jesus." I adjusted myself, the hard-on I was sporting making my world close in on nothing but Zuri. And that hot as fuck car.

"Do you want to take her for a spin?" Zuri held the keys in the air, a teasing smile on her face.

"Fuck yes." My voice came out more growl than I'd intended, but I couldn't hold it back. The car...the woman... the fact that we were alone but could be interrupted at any moment. It was all one big fantasy coming true.

"Well." Zuri licked her lips and gave me a look that made me want to throw her down on the hood and plant my face between her legs. "Hop in, Phoenix."

A chill shivered down my spine. This woman was such a mind-fuck. Soft and sweet and girly, but driving a badass muscle car and being all sex-kitten with me. I had no idea what I'd done to deserve such a gift, but I was never going to take it, or her, for granted.

I stalked toward Zuri slowly, my eyes staying on hers no matter how much I wanted to check out the car. Her lips turned up in a teasing smile, one that spoke of the dirty things I knew she had to be thinking about. I gripped her hips when I reached her, pulling her toward me, desperate for her touch. My wolf spirit was practically panting, almost out of control with lust.

"Zuri, I'm so…"

She put a finger against my lips, her smirk turning positively wicked. "Get in, baby."

Stepping out of my arms, she dropped the keys in my hand and walked around the back of the car to the passenger side. Swinging her hips in a way that made my balls ache even more. I took a deep breath before opening the door and dropping into the driver's seat.

"Fuck me," I groaned as my ass hit the upholstery. The seat was pushed all the way back, which I thought odd. Zuri was shorter than I was, and even with my long legs, I would need to pull the seat forward to be able to drive.

But then my mate—my sexy, naughty, wicked mate— whispered, "I'd love to."

That was my only warning before Zuri launched herself across the divide between the seats to straddle my lap. I grabbed her hips as her mouth landed on mine, sliding my tongue inside with a groan. She responded to my kiss as she settled herself squarely on my dick. The weight of her, the heat, had me growling and clutching her to me.

"Missed you," she whispered between kisses. I grunted my agreement, too focused on her lips to comment. Her body undulated against me as we kissed, the heat from her pussy obvious even through my jeans. I wanted to feel that heat on my fingers, my lips, my dick. Wanted to slide inside her right there, sitting in the driver's seat of her Camaro.

My hands couldn't stay still. I grabbed, kneaded, slid, gripped…I wanted her closer. Wanted to surround myself with her. Wanted to feel every inch of her. As if understanding my greediness, she unzipped her heavy winter coat and caught my hands, dragging them under her sweater and up to her breasts. Soft, full, and so very heavy, even more so than I remembered. But it'd been so long, too many days since I'd held them. I needed time and access to relearn. Rememorize.

I groaned and nipped her lip as I palmed her, rolling her nipple with my other hand. "Zuri."

She shook her head as she unzipped my coat then brought her frantic hands between us.

"I don't want slow or sweet." Her husky voice went right to my cock, and she moaned as I pushed up into her again. "I need you so much, Phoenix. Please."

I nodded as she unzipped my jeans, lifting my hips so she could wiggle the fabric far enough down my legs to pull out my dick. Her hot hands on me made my eyes roll back in my head. So much pleasure. One stroke, two, a thumb over the tip. My head hit the headrest as I let loose a loud growl at the feel of her gripping me, working me. Fuck, she'd make me come within seconds if she kept it up. But suddenly those amazing hands were gone. With a whimper, I glanced down in time to watch her pull her skirt up around her hips, my eyes nearly bugging out at what I saw.

"Fuck…no panties?" I traced a finger along the groove near her hipbone, loving how soft she felt. "Someone was planning this."

She gave me a smirk. "I've been practically dripping for you all day."

I growled and yanked her to me, owning her mouth as I slid one hand between us. Holy fuck, was she soaked. Hot, wet, and swollen-with-need flesh met my fingers. She groaned and threw her head back as I rubbed my finger over her clit, her hands fisting the leather of my Feral Breed jacket.

"Don't tease me," she whispered, moving her hips against my hand.

"Never, baby." I leaned forward to bite that plump bottom lip of hers and slid two fingers inside. "Damn. You're so ready."

"Been ready." She lifted herself up, just enough for me to see the sheen of her arousal coating my hand. I wanted to taste it. Wanted her in my mouth and riding my face. But that would have to come later, maybe in the backseat. Because being in her car made everything between us that much more intense. A mechanic and a sexy gearhead. Fucking perfect.

I gripped my dick and ran the head over her clit, teasing her for a few passes before sliding against her opening. Thrusting up as she dropped down on me. Tight, slow, and hot.

We both whispered a reverent *fuck* when I slid all the way inside. I had to go still for a moment to enjoy that initial sensation, to not come before she was ready. The burn of her heat, the grip of her walls around me made it difficult to stay in control.

And then my mate began to fuck me.

Up and down, back and forth, circling her hips, forcing me to follow her lead. She worked herself on me, running the show. And I loved every fucking second of it. She'd never been this forward before. She wasn't shy about her needs, but this was different. This was more direct.

This was her taking her pleasure from me, no holds barred.

As the tingle in my balls grew, I reached between us and pressed the side of my finger against her clit. I needed her to come first, had to push her over that edge before I could surrender to it. And I was already so fucking close.

She shivered and groaned as I massaged that magic little spot. I stopped only to bring my finger to my mouth, sucking it in, licking off her juices and wetting my skin before returning to my job of getting her off.

"C'mon, baby." I grunted as I met each of her thrusts with one of my own. "Want to feel you come on me. Need to." I gripped her thigh with my hand, helping guide her movements. "Fuck, you're so beautiful. How'd I ever get so damn lucky?"

Zuri slowed her pace, her eyes opening and a sweet smile creeping across her lips even as she continued riding me. She leaned forward and placed a gentle kiss on my mouth before whispering, "I'm the lucky one here."

She kissed me hard and deep as she swiveled those hips of hers, drawing me in. I didn't think anything could feel as good as her body wrapped around mine, but this? This was pure heaven. A little risk of being caught, the confined space of the car's interior, and my baby working my dick like it was the last chance we'd ever have to be this close. She was blowing my lust up to epic proportions.

"So good," I whispered. "You feel so good. I've missed this. Needed it." I lifted my hips, pulling her down to go a little deeper, get a little more. "So hungry for you, baby."

Zuri groaned and circled her hips harder, faster. "Gonna come, Adam. So close…so much."

I growled and thrust into her, doing my best to get her to that point. To make her come. There was nothing I wanted more. Nothing that would satisfy me the way her walls clamping around my dick would right then. Just a little more. A bit harder. A tilt of her hips. A pinch of her clit.

Within seconds, she was fluttering around my dick, her breath catching as her orgasm took hold. And when she came, when she shattered right there in my lap, it was with my name on her lips. My real one.

"Adam, Adam. Yes."

"Fuck," I hissed as I followed her, coming with a shiver and a deep groan. Putting reality on hold as we rode out our tiny deaths.

She clung to me as we calmed, her breathing slowing to a normal pace before mine did. And then she laughed.

"Well, that was a first."

I kissed the top of her head and ran my hands up her back, still desperate to feel her skin. "What was a first?"

"Sex in my Camaro."

I chuckled as she licked a path up my neck. "Really? This car is sex on legs; I figured you had plenty of opportunity."

"Oh, I had opportunity. I just never wanted to partake."

She looked up at me and grinned. "No one else has ever been worth risking my upholstery."

I laughed, loud and ringing in the small space. Zuri did the same, the two of us shaking and hugging and being altogether couple-ish as we sat half-naked in the front seat of her Camaro. A perfect moment, even if it was a bit cold.

When we finally stopped laughing, she pulled herself off me and sat up in my lap. "I've got towels in the backseat."

"That's it?" I raised my eyebrows and gave her my best fake surprised face. "No romance? No afterglow or cuddling? Just a wham bam thank you…sir?"

Zuri gave me a look that clearly said she thought I was being a smartass. I grinned back, knowing she was right.

"First, it's fucking freezing out here. Second, this steering wheel is digging into my back. And third"—she leaned forward, bringing her lips to my ear—"the sooner we get to your apartment, the sooner you get to fuck me in your bed, on your couch, in your shower, on your kitchen table, against your—"

"Our." I stopped her with a deep, soul-shaking kiss before pushing her off my lap and carefully placing her in the passenger seat. "Our bed, our couch, our shower, under our Christmas tree, and on top of our kitchen table. Now quit talking and grab the towels. I want to get you home."

"Sure thing, Adam." Her return grin was the stuff sappy love songs were written about, and I basked in it as she said my favorite words in the world.

"Let's go home."

CHRISTMAS WITH REBEL

Rebel & Charlotte
December: Takes Place Shortly After *The Car Revealed*

Rebel

"What did you get him?"

I hummed, ignoring Charlotte's question. I knew what she'd say when she found out what my Christmas gift to Julian had been. She was going to tear me a new one. But the boy was a teenager, and I was the only male figure in his life. It was my job to make sure he was ready for adulthood.

"Rebel?"

"Yeah, kitten?"

"What did you get Julian for Christmas?"

I grabbed her and pulled her into my arms, manhandling her until we were standing under the mistletoe in the entryway. My only addition to her holiday decorations. I'd thought it would be a fun and sexy way to keep my mate on her toes, though it was working in an ass-saving capacity just fine as well.

"Let's not talk about Julian right now." I kissed her good and deep, pulling her close. She melted into my hold, sliding her tongue against mine. But just when I thought I might be getting a little under-the-tree action—

Charlotte grabbed my ear and pulled, stopping the kiss mid-stroke and glaring at me. "What did you do?"

"Nothing," I tried to pull away but she held tight, yanking me down to her eye level.

"Abraham Lynch, I swear, if you bought him some kind of weapon or something—"

"Easy, Char," Julian said, interrupting her interrogation as he appeared at the bottom of the stairs. "He didn't buy me the flamethrower I asked for, promise."

As soon as Charlotte released my ear, I jumped back, intending to keep out of her reach when Julian spilled the beans.

"What did he get you then?" Charlotte asked, crossing her arms over her chest and watching her brother.

Julian shrugged and shuffled toward the kitchen. "He got me a subscription to an audiobook site."

My jaw popped open at the slight twist to the truth, but I quickly shut it and did my best to look innocent before I busted myself. Charlotte turned, disbelief on her face.

"Audiobooks?"

I shrugged, mimicking Julian's casualness. "Everyone needs a little fiction in their life."

She squinted, turning back around as Julian came back through the entryway, can of soda in hand.

"What kind of books are these?"

"Fantasy, mostly," Julian said, not even stopping on his way back to his room.

"Fantasy? Like Lord of the Rings?" Charlotte asked.

"Yeah, sure. There's rings."

I choked back a snort, trying to disguise it as a cough.

Julian paused as he reached the stairs, turning toward us, his unseeing eyes directed over my shoulder. "Thanks, by the way, Rebel. I really do appreciate the gift."

"No problem, man." I smiled as he climbed the stairs. "You gonna join us for lunch?"

"Nope." I heard his door open. "I'm…not feeling well. I'm

just going to hang out in my room for a while."

I smirked, knowing exactly what he was going to be doing in his room.

"Just yell if you need anything," Charlotte said, turning back to face me. I raised my eyebrow, waiting. Finally she huffed. "Fine. I'm sorry. When you wouldn't tell me what you bought him, I assumed it was something you didn't want me to know about."

I wrapped her up in my arms again, dragging her back under the mistletoe. "Why do you always think the worst of me?"

"Because you prove me right ninety-nine percent of the time." Her words were sarcastic—and probably true—but at least she said them with a smile on her lips. Speaking of lips, she pressed hers to mine, just once, a soft kiss that still sent all my blood south. Groaning, I pulled her tighter, pushing my cock against her hip and sliding my hands under her sweater.

Charlotte jumped as the sound of some kind of heavy rock music blared through the house, and then she sighed and pulled away.

"Well that's the end of that," she whispered.

Growling, my need to be inside her at a peak I wasn't willing to back away from just yet, I picked her up and tossed her over my shoulder, heading for the stairs. "Nope, that's just the beginning."

"Rebel," she said, laughing. "What are you doing?"

"Taking advantage of your brother's distractions." I carried her up the stairs, slamming her bedroom door closed behind me.

"What if he hears us?" She asked as I set her on the ground. I shook my head, stripping her sweater off.

"He's got that damn music so loud, he wouldn't hear a jet plane landing on the house."

Charlotte glanced toward the door as if nervous, but her

nipples were hard and her heart was racing. She was just as horny as I was.

"What if he needs me?"

I snorted, knowing exactly how little her brother needed Charlotte right at that moment. "He won't need you."

She finally looked my way, desire winning out over her reservations. I unhooked her red lace bra—merry Christmas to me—and tossed it across the room. One little bite to her bottom lip, a single nip, and I dropped to my knees, wrapping my lips around a nipple. Suckling her, nibbling, teasing. She sighed, her fingers fisting in my hair as I unbuttoned her pants.

"What if—"

"He won't need you," I said, interrupting her and blowing across her wet flesh before moving to the other breast. "He's got enough to keep him busy."

Once I had her naked, I tossed her on the bed and crawled between her legs. Afternoon sex with my mate while her brother was home was something I'd never managed to have. We always had to wait for alone time or for the early-morning hours when we knew he was asleep. While I loved the kid like he was my own brother, the fact was I wanted more time with Charlotte. Adult time…naked time.

Hence the Christmas gift.

As I slid inside my mate, dropping my head to her shoulder and biting my lip to savor that first push into her wet heat, I sent up a silent thanks. Thanks for hard rock music, thanks for loud speakers, thanks for the internet and Google, and a special thanks to the creator of the present I'd gotten Julian for Christmas. Who knew buying him a subscription to a website that streamed audio files of professionally read, hard-core erotica would get me laid?

BITCHES DON'T RIDE

Gates & Kaija

January: Takes Place Between *Claiming His Witch* & *Claiming His Beauty*

Gates

"Feral Breed Four Corners, what say ye?"

The president of the den stood and nodded his respect. I sat with Scab and Rebel, waiting for our turn at roll call. Blaze, National President of the Feral Breed and leader of the National Association of the Lycan Brotherhood, stood at the lectern, looking down at his papers. His new mate sat at his right, a shewolf named Moira from some pack in the Appalachian Mountains. Blaze's eyes kept dropping to her, a nervous tic that most of the men in the room probably didn't even notice. I only did because I understood it. He wasn't comfortable with her in the room, exposed to the possibility of danger.

As head of the ruling party of all shifters in North America, Blaze was used to dealing with men who would eventually decide to take him out and claim the leadership spot from under him. I couldn't see a den president of the Feral Breed going for the jugular like that—not for a job dealing with all the ridiculous pack politicos and their warped notions of what tradition meant.

Still, I couldn't blame him for his protectiveness. I was experiencing a similar anxiety.

My eyes wandered to the rear door of the hall. To where my mate was hidden, waiting. I could feel her back there, her nerves and her tenacity. We were introducing Kaija to the Breed leadership today, plus informing them that our den was riding with four mated wolves. Rebel had already told Blaze our updates, and we'd brought along a larger group of denmates than we normally would, just in case there was trouble. The men in this room were old school, claiming the only place a woman had in the Breed was as someone's bike bunny or old lady. Not a mate, not a member. Things were about to get interesting.

"What ever happened to that douchenozzle, Jameson?" Scab asked.

Rebel set his beer down and turned in his seat, facing Scab. "Rumor has it Jameson's either on a special mission for Blaze or serving some kind of punishment for endangering the secret, though no one knows for sure. Next meeting will be a year since we saw him."

Scab huffed. "Yeah, I remember."

I hummed and grinned, remembering how Jameson had laid Scab flat for making crass comments about another shifter and his mate. That was before Rebel met Charlotte, the first of our den to find his mate. Phoenix and I had been blessed with our fated ones mere months later.

My eyes slid once more to Blaze's new mate. She was a pretty wolf, no doubt about that, but it was the aura of calm surrounding her that spoke to me. She sat in front of a room full of Alpha men in her business skirt and her button-down shirt as if she belonged there. There was no fear on her face, no fidgeting. Just Moira with her glasses on and her laptop open, typing away the minutes of the meeting. Completely ignoring the way the men in the room whispered and stared.

"Think you can handle this?" Rebel asked, keeping his voice low as he leaned toward me.

I gave him a sidelong glance. "Think you can?"

He chuffed and shook his head. "Fuck no, but I'm going balls to the wall on this one. I just hope our brothers behave themselves. Looks like Blaze is already about to tear into a few hides."

He glanced around the room, taking in the head nods some of the men were making toward Moira and the rude hand gestures. Fuck me, if they tried that shit with my Kaija, I'd rip off their arms, which was exactly what couldn't happen. I needed to collar my wolf spirit and settle my instincts. I knew getting these men to accept my mate as a Feral Breed member wasn't going to be easy, but I couldn't make it worse by jumping to her defense at every crack. She was going to have to stand up on her own if she intended to prove herself to these animals. I knew that, she knew that…we just had to stick to our plan.

"Feral Breed Detroit, what say ye?"

Rebel shot me a warning look then stood and nodded his respect to Blaze. "We lost a longtime member this past year. While in the end, the man had lost control of his wolf spirit and had fallen too far past the feral line, he'd lived a long life as a productive member of the Breed. His passing deserves our respect. My den is in mourning for our fallen brother, Spook."

Bottles were raised all around, the other dens showing their respect for a fallen comrade. Spook had come close to killing Rebel last month, and his actions had caused Phoenix quite a bit of trouble as well, but he was still our brethren. He'd fought by our sides many times. Losing control of your human mind and going feral was just part of the life of an unmated shifter. A sad reality I'd never been more grateful to have escaped by meeting Kaija.

After a moment of silence, Blaze nodded his approval. "May brother Spook find peace in the afterlife." He glanced back at his papers, endlessly flipping from page to page. "And your overall membership numbers?"

"Up one. Balancing out the loss of Spook is a prospect promoted in November. Phoenix has officially been patched into the Detroit Den. We also picked up a new member, bringing our headcount into the positive. On the advice of our Sergeant-at-Arms, we are putting the warehouse in southwest Detroit up for sale. There's no need to have two buildings within the same city." Rebel paused. Anyone else wouldn't have thought much about it, but I'd known the man for a long time. He was taking a moment to settle his wolf in case things got rowdy. I forced my ass back in my seat and lounged against the wall. Slouching. Casual. Completely at ease.

Giving off an impression that was the opposite of what I was feeling inside.

"On another note," Rebel said, his voice strong and smooth, "Feral Breed Detroit now rides with four mated wolves."

The room went silent. Every hair on the back of my neck stood on end as the tension rose, but I kept up my nonchalant act. Let the weaker wolves start the fight. I'd be the one to finish it if need be.

"Mated wolves don't ride," someone shouted from the other side of the room. Before Rebel or Blaze could answer, Moira stood, demanding our attention with her no-bullshit expression.

"There is no official rule banning mated shifters from joining or riding with the Feral Breed. If the shifter in question earns their patch and upholds the standards of the den, being mated doesn't risk their membership in the national club."

Blaze smirked as she reclaimed her seat, giving her a look filled with such heat and passion it nearly scorched the podium. Everyone in this room knew Moira was actually his second mate, the only female in their powerful Alpha triad. What we hadn't known was what she was like, but we did now. The woman had balls to stand up in front of our group and argue a point of club regulations. Big brass ones.

Before the other wolves could lose their shit over the issue of riding while mated, Blaze called for Rebel's attention.

"Tell me more about your newly patched member, Phoenix."

Rebel nodded. "He's been known by members of our den since he was given his wolf spirit ten years ago by the Beast, and he was a hanger-on for over a year before we accepted him as a prospect. Phoenix is well liked by the rest of the den. He's honest, a hard worker, and he earned his patch honorably."

"He's mated to a witch, is that correct?" Blaze glanced up, his face filled with curiosity.

"Yes, sir." Once again, the room stilled. Rebel ignored the heavy silence, staying focused on Blaze, though I could see the way his shoulders had stiffened. Wolves and witches didn't normally mingle. To this group, the stakes had just been raised.

Blaze leaned on the podium and cocked his head. "What category of magick does she practice?"

"She's an elemental witch, sir. Water magick, to be precise. Her sisters are air and fire witches, and the three of them use Phoenix to balance the four elements, as our wolf spirits mimic their earth element."

The chattering of the wolves in the room started small—a few whispers here and there—but then it swelled, filling the room with the sound of fearful and disgruntled men voicing their disgust. But at the first witch slur used, Blaze slammed his fist against the podium.

"I understand the Detroit den is doing things a little differently than most, but that doesn't mean you can disrespect my meeting and my den president with your petty arguments. The woman is a mate to one of your brothers, and she will be treated with respect both in word and in deed. If you have a valid reason why the den shouldn't be associating with witches, you can make an appointment with Half Trac to speak with me." Blaze paused, glaring out over the crowd, his Alpha power positively stifling the energy of the room. "I believe we'll be letting him out of solitary confinement in another six months or so, though any one of you is more than welcome to join him."

The men in the room quieted at the reminder of the harsh punishments Blaze handed out. Not as physically severe as some of the past National Presidents, who'd simply kill a wolf for a single transgression. No, Blaze was more creative, while also believing in penance. Half Trac had ignored Blaze's orders and acted on his own during a mission, which had almost cost me the life of my mate. I hated the fucker for it, so I saw Blaze's solitary confinement punishment as earned and appropriate. The other wolves, being that we were all such social creatures in spirit, probably saw it as a living hell. Whatever. The guy earned his time.

"Back to my Detroit den"—he raised an eyebrow at Rebel—"or rather, your Detroit den."

Rebel chuckled and shook his head. "I make no claim over yours, sir."

Blaze gave him a tiny smirk before looking down at his papers. "We have Phoenix as a newly patched member, but you also have a new prospect."

"Technically a prospect, though not one tagged as a Pup. They earned an honorary road name while working with the Valkoisus pack a few months back."

"Road name already." Blaze shook his head, writing something down as he clicked his tongue. "You do like to skirt the rules out there in Detroit, don't you?"

Rebel glanced at me with a smirk before turning to face the podium once more.

"It's the blue collar in us, sir." When Blaze looked up, Rebel gave him a cheeky grin. "Let other people worry about rules and regulations. We prefer to get shit done."

The room echoed with the grunts and chuffs of other shifters based in hard-working, blue-collar towns. There'd always been a bit of a good-natured rivalry between us and the dens in more affluent areas, the Hollywood den being at the top of that list. Blaze didn't let the ribbing last too long, though. Soon enough, he called the room to order.

"I'd like to meet this new prospect." His eyes nearly twinkled as he stared at Rebel. "Is he here with us?"

"Well, kind of."

I brought my beer to my lips to hide my smile. The old codger. Blaze knew our prospect was a woman, but he was setting this up to be quite the announcement. I had a feeling he was challenging the men in the room, daring them to overreact. I let my weight fall back onto my hips and gripped the side of the table, just in case. I would not be the one to fail his little test.

Rebel took a step back to clear an aisle, coming to stand directly beside me before giving two loud barks. The back doors to the room flew open, a wall of denim and black leather making its way through the crowd. At the front, forming the tip of the spear so to speak, was my mate. All five-foot-nothing of her, with her white-blonde hair tied up in a ponytail and her face bare of any makeup. She was the most beautiful thing I'd ever seen, sexy in an understated way that appealed to me. Plus, she walked in as if she owned the room. Head high, gait sure, tight-as-fuck leather pants drawing the eyes of every male in the room. My girl was not going to let these men scare her.

Damn if that confidence didn't make me hard.

Rebel gestured toward our crew as he addressed the room. "I give you Phoenix, who earned his patch by always acting with the best interest of the club at heart. He worked for those colors, battling a magickal cocktail we'd never experienced and fighting his way back from the dead, quite literally. We're proud of him and ask that you give him a hearty Feral Breed welcome. As for our prospect"—his hand landed on Kaija's shoulder— "please meet Princess, who—"

Rebel was unable finish his introduction as the room exploded in sound. Shifters yelled and growled, voicing their displeasure over a female Breed member. I sat back, cracking the tabletop I clung to and working hard to keep myself in check. I wanted to protect my mate, to stand between her and the threat these men posed, but I couldn't. I knew that, and she knew that. Kaija would have to earn her place in the Breed, and that started by not needing her mate to stand up for her.

As the insults and slurs started flying our way, my denmates drew in tighter, supporting their newest member. They'd taken to my mate, some even surprising me with how well they accepted her. Like Scab, who stood a step behind Kaija, glaring at each den president in turn.

"Bitches don't ride," someone yelled.

"What are we, the tampon brigade?" another called.

But the one that made me almost jump out of my chair was when a shifter from Boston hollered, "The only way a bitch should be riding with the Breed is on the back or on my cock. You up for it, sweetheart?"

My claws sank into the wood table as I swallowed a growl, but it was Scab who answered. He barked three times, quieting the men in the room before turning a wicked glare on the Boston shifter and snarling his displeasure. The man stared back, obviously surprised to be challenged by the Detroit shifter.

"It's okay," Kaija whispered to Scab, touching his arm for just a moment to help calm him. She took a deep breath and stepped forward, her head high, no fear on her face. "My name is Kaija Wariksen, formerly of the Valkoisus pack. I was given the road name Princess after fighting alongside the Detroit den, though I'm unpatched. I'm also mated to my denmate, the Gatekeeper."

The room went completely still as all eyes turned my way. The fucker from Boston with the crass mouth visibly paled, his surprise quickly sliding into fear. I grinned and leaned back against the wall before lifting my beer in a mock salute, working hard for that don't-give-a-shit vibe. After a moment of tense silence—as every shifter in the room waited for me to do something other than sit there and drink—Blaze tapped his podium to get our attention.

"Welcome, Princess. I look forward to watching you earn your Feral Breed place."

"Thank you, sir. I look forward to earning it." Kaija nodded her respect, having been instructed on how to behave by Rebel before the meeting. Pride soared through me as our leader smiled at her, completely charmed by my girl.

As soon as Blaze moved on to the next den, Kaija turned with our denmates to leave. On the way to the door, some fucker snuck up and grabbed her ass. My feet hit the floor before he'd even let go of her flesh, not that she needed me. Kaija spun at the offending touch, grabbing his wrist and twisting as she delivered three quick kicks to his abdomen and ribs. The man went down with a crash, clutching his arm.

"You broke my wrist, you bitch."

Rebel and Numbers flanked Kaija as Scab stepped up to the fallen shifter.

"She's not the one crying on the ground, son. So who's the bitch?"

Kaija caught my eye for a tiny moment, giving me just enough of a head shake for me to understand. I sat back in my chair once more, fighting my every instinct as I let her run the show. She stood tall and looked around the room. Every eye was on her again; even Moira had stood from her spot to watch the spectacle. But Kaija didn't show weakness. My sweet girl had a badass side the men in this room would have to learn about quickly if they didn't want to end up on their asses.

"Anyone else want to go?" Kaija asked, her back straight and her gaze filled with steely fury. When she received no answers, she huffed and turned. But before she left, she glared down at the man who'd dared to lay a hand on her. "You got lucky on that grab, but know this—if you ever touch me again, I'll kill you myself."

Pride. It filled me, made me want to grab my mate and kiss her until she knew how much she'd just accomplished. By successfully defending herself, she'd shown the club that she was more than capable of handling at least some of the physical requirements of our jobs. That kick and her brazen attitude would go a long way toward getting the other dens to accept her.

Kaija tossed me a wink before walking out the door with the rest of our group, her hips swinging in those painted-on leather pants. Fuck, she was so damn hot.

Wishing for a quick end to roll call so I could get a little alone time with my mate, I glanced up at the podium. A smirk rested upon Moira's face while Blaze watched Kaija leave with a small smile on his. Yeah, my girl had done good. And I couldn't wait to reward her.

Kaija

My hands shook and my heart pounded as I walked out of the meeting room, but I did my best to hide it from my denmates. Phoenix knew, though. The boy—well, man, seeing as how he was mated and all—had a way of seeing to the heart of things and breaking down whatever defenses you put up. And he was watching me closely as I struggled to come to grips with the damage I'd done.

"The chump deserved it," Phoenix said, as if he could hear my thoughts.

"He deserved his arm broken? Because that's what I did. I broke him." My stomach churned at the memory. Damn, I hadn't meant to break his bones. That twist and kick move was one I'd been using against my brothers for decades. But my brothers were bigger and brawnier than the jerk, and I hadn't adjusted for his size. That fact made my chest tighten and my stomach clench. I hadn't meant to really hurt him.

"You didn't break him." Phoenix smiled at me as he pulled his phone out of his pocket. "Besides, he really did deserve it. You didn't do anything wrong; his wandering hands being where they shouldn't be did. He should be thankful it was you that handled the situation. Could you imagine what Gates wanted to do to him?"

I bit back a smile, trying to quell the arousal building inside of me. My Gates may have kept his butt in his chair as we'd demanded him to do in case anything had gone wrong, but his eyes had betrayed his rage. That look had lit a fire inside of me. One that only he could put out.

"My mate is very protective of me."

"Understatement, Princess." Phoenix snorted and started tapping on his phone, his smile falling to a frown.

"What's wrong?" I asked.

"Uh…Zuri's sick." He shook his head as he finished his message.

"Oh, I'm sorry to hear that."

"Yeah." He bit his lip, still staring at his phone. "Scarlett's taking care of her at our place, so I know she's okay. I just…"

When he trailed off, I placed a hand on his arm. "You want to be there to take care of her and see for yourself that she's okay."

He paused then nodded slowly.

I grinned. "Guess Gates isn't the only overprotective male in the club."

Before he could answer, the denmates who'd been participating in the roll call meeting came striding through the door. Well, most of them.

"Where's Rebel?" Phoenix asked, even as my eyes searched

for Gates.

"He's got to stay until the end, but he told all of us to go on and head out," Scab said. He looked to Numbers, his roommate on this trip. "Want to head into the city for a bit? We can hit up Rush Street or something."

"Sure," Numbers said with a shrug. He hurried over to grab my forearm, a respectful custom in the shifter world. "You did great in there. Congratulations."

"Thank you." I smiled and turned to Scab. "And thank you for quieting the ruckus."

He eyed me hard, a wicked grin curling one side of his mouth. "You're *our* bitch, Princess. Everyone else can just sit back and wish they were able to look at you in leather all day."

"Jesus, Scab." Numbers grabbed the other shifter by the arm and tugged him out the door.

"Those two are going to end up in jail," Phoenix whispered. He put his phone away and turned toward the open doors just as Gates walked through them. "Hey, man. Rebel's heading up to Milwaukee to see Charlotte as soon as he's done in there, and Scab and Numbers are headed downtown to get into trouble. Zuri's sick, so I'm going to call a cab and head to the airport."

Tearing my eyes away from my mate, who had yet to even blink as he stared at me, I gave the young shifter a smile. When I raised an eyebrow, he smiled, looking sheepish.

"I know. Overprotective. But she's my world"—he shrugged—"there's nothing I wouldn't do for her."

I nodded, understanding. "Go. Take care of your lady."

Once he walked away, I slowly turned to my mate. He stood stock-still six feet away, staring at me. His body practically frozen in place. But there was a fire in his eyes. A need.

"Gates?"

He shivered, a low growl rising in his chest. More men came out of the meeting room, though not ones I knew. Not ones from our den. They leered at me, their eyes traveling the length of my body and making me feel the desire to curl in on myself. Gates' growl grew louder and deeper even as he continued to watch me. The anger there, the threat, made the hair on my arms stand on end. The men must have realized the danger they were in because they took the hint and hurried off to… someplace else.

"Lorenz—"

"Come. Now." Gates grabbed my arm and led me away from the meeting room. He strode deep into the labyrinth of hallways that made up the mansion known as Merriweather Fields. Without a word, we rushed past multiple doors, up two flights of stairs, and made a number of turns until I felt completely disoriented. All the while, Gates growled and breathed heavily, making my body practically quiver in anticipation. He was angry and impatient, but not with me. Never with me. This was in reaction to those other men. The possessive side of my mate making its presence known.

Finally, Gates threw open a nondescript door in a hallway lined with more of the same. He pulled me inside, immediately shoving me into the wall as he slammed the door behind us. And then he was there. His entire body pressed against me, his lips almost brushing mine, his mouth stealing my breath, and the hard line of his erection pressing against my hip.

"Fuck, baby," he whispered, the sound more growl than voice. "I thought I was going to kill that man."

Though I knew exactly the person he spoke about, I still asked, "Which man?"

"The one who dared to touch you. To touch what's mine." His hand moved between us, agile fingers unsnapping my pants and lowering the zipper. "All those men who were watching you, leering at you."

"Yours," I whispered, knowing exactly what he needed. Gates nodded even as he continued to growl, running his lips up my neck and then rubbing his cheek against mine.

"Again."

I shivered when he bit my earlobe, the feel of his teeth on my skin immediately making me wet. "Yours."

This time, he moved to my neck. Biting harder, making my body arch into his as I gasped.

"Again." His voice was louder this time, more direct and demanding. More arousing.

"Yours." Trembling, knees barely strong enough to hold myself up, I gave myself over to the sensations he created within me. From the way his breath teased my skin to the pleasure-pain of his teeth burying themselves in my flesh. The need and desire he instilled as he rocked his hips into me. Fuck, he was so sexy like this. So desperate to prove something that didn't need proving. But I let him, encouraged him even, because I liked it when he lost control.

With a snarled "Mine," he spun me, pressing my chest against the wall. I gasped and wriggled as one of his large hands came to hold me by my throat. Trapping me with his grip and his body. Owning me. His other hand dipped low, sliding into my pants to find me soaking wet. Ready for him. Always and only for him.

He growled in my ear as his fingers honed in on my clit, circling the tender flesh with the perfect amount of pressure. I whined and mewled, my body tensing as I tried to move. But Gates had me completely at his mercy, and he knew it.

"Your ass looks fucking delicious in these pants." He pinched my clit, making me groan long and loud as my pussy clenched on nothing. Empty. Damn, I felt so empty.

"I know. You tell me that every time I wear them." I put a little growl in my voice and pushed back against him, pretending to try to escape his hold. He tightened his grip and continued playing with me, knowing how much I loved his dominance.

"Tease," he growled as his fingers thrust inside. I moaned, spreading my legs wider and pressing my ass against his dick.

He chuckled and squeezed my throat just a little, barely enough to force my head higher.

I ground against him. "I'd never tease you."

As his fingers and thumb took care of my needy pussy, he moved my head back. Gently, more guiding than pulling, exposing more of my neck.

"Mine," he growled, licking down my shoulder to the claiming scar he'd given me little more than a month ago. Damn, we'd been together every day since, finding pleasure with each other multiple times a day as we learned each other's likes and limits. But this, this full-scale domination of my body, was new. And I fucking loved it.

"Yours."

Gates snarled, the fingers in my pussy pumping faster, his thumb more aggressive in the pressure against my clit. I groaned and put both hands against the wall, needing it for support as my approaching orgasm grew inside of me. Tension curled low in my belly, and a need for more and faster and harder made my body arch and bow. Nothing but want. Desire. His fingers. His mouth.

When Gates' teeth covered my claiming bite, I shivered. When his breath rushed against my wet skin, I moaned. And when his whispered "Mine" met my ears, I shook and gasped.

"Yours." My hips rocked against his hand, no longer under my control. I was all sensation and instinct, chasing an orgasm that was barreling toward me like a freight train.

"Mine." His proclamation was a harsh bark of sound, one that made me clench around his fingers. He followed it up by biting over my claiming mark, reclaiming me. I came with a shout, trembling in his arms as he used his body weight to pin me to the wall.

"Yours, yours," I cried, not caring about volume or if anyone was close enough to hear me. All I knew was Gates, all I felt was his hand milking the last drop of pleasure from me.

"Always yours."

The way he roared as I came around his fingers shook the door and made me shiver in pleasure. With little fanfare, Gates spun me and picked me up, tossing me over his shoulder. He crossed to the bed in three quick steps then threw me down on the mattress.

"Take them off," he growled, his eyes on my legs. "Take them off before I tear them from your body."

I smirked and crawled up to my knees. Finger trailing the waistband of my leather pants, I whispered, "These?"

Gates' returning growl grew louder, coarser. I yanked my shirt over my head and removed my bra with a flick of my wrist. Lying back on the mattress, I inched the leather down my legs, loving the heated stare he gave me as he stood at the end of the bed. Once naked and ready, I relaxed into the mattress, cocked my head, and spread my legs for him.

"Like this?"

He stared at my pussy, drinking me in, memorizing every inch. Feeling powerful and a bit naughty, I traced my fingers down to run slowly along the side of my pussy. Teasing myself. Sliding along the swollen flesh.

Before I could do much more than a single pass, Gates was on me. He didn't even bother to undress, just shoved his pants down far enough to expose his long, thick dick.

"Mine."

"Yours," I practically purred, ready and willing to prove it. But there was nothing for me to do. Gates slid inside me with a single thrust, immediately setting a brutal pace. The harshness of his movements wasn't lost on me, and the need to be claimed by him was something I welcomed. Being possessed and possessive was something we both understood.

"Fuck, Kaija." Gates' head hit my shoulder, his growl now a sustained thing. I held him close, ran my fingers through his hair, and wrapped my legs around his hips.

"I know. It's okay. I know."

He whimpered and jerked, his rhythm faltering. Four more thrusts and he froze, his body tense with the release his orgasm brought. His roar of completion making the door shake on its hinges again.

"Fuck." He dropped on top of me, his weight pinning me to the bed. I ran my hands up and down his back, loving the way he made me feel so small and delicate underneath him. But then he whispered, "I'm sorry."

I pulled back, hoping to make eye contact. "For what?"

"For...everything." He leaned up on one arm, meeting my confused gaze. "For not helping you down there, and for feeling the need to help you when I know you can handle yourself. For attacking you as soon as we walked in. For not giving you a second"—he pressed a soft kiss to my lips—"or a third"—another kiss—"or a fourth orgasm before I finished."

I chuckled. "You're not some kind of superhero."

"Hey." He pouted, that bottom lip completely adorable.

"Fine," I said as I rolled my eyes. "You're the biggest, baddest superhero ever, and I'm lucky to even be in your presence."

He grinned, making his blue eyes crinkle at the corners. "You're ridiculous."

"And you're too hard on yourself." I curled to my side when he dropped onto the mattress beside me. This time the quiet lasted longer, the two of us wrapped around each other. Until I couldn't hold in my worries any longer.

"You know it's not going to stop."

"I know." He sighed and pulled me in tighter. "I hate how they stare at you."

"And I hate knowing it bothers you. But, Gates?"

"Hmmm?"

"It doesn't bother me. They don't matter—their stares don't matter. Even that guy grabbing my ass didn't matter. Because deep down, I know exactly where I belong and who actually does matter."

He smiled, one so beautiful it made my heart ache. "You mean me, right?"

"Yes, you silly man."

I giggled as he tugged me on top of him, spreading my legs over his hips. He pushed my hair over my shoulders as I leaned down to capture a kiss, one hand going to the back of my neck to hold me in place. When he finally released my lips, he gazed up at me with a look so warm and filled with love, it made my heart leap in my chest.

"I am so fucking lucky I found you."

I melted at his words, so honest and open. So true in more ways than he intended.

"We're both the lucky ones."

As I lifted up to help him slide inside of me, I kept my eyes on his. Showing him how much I loved him. Speaking without sound. Promising without words.

Mine.

Yours.

Ours.

Forever.

DOMESTICATION

Phoenix & Azurine

February: Takes Place During *Claiming His Beauty*

Azurine

"You feeling okay, Zuri?" Phoenix glanced at me before turning to watch the road once more. "Your motion sickness getting to you again?"

"I guess." I closed my eyes as I clung to the door handle. "Just a little queasy."

Queasy was an understatement. I was in a total anxiety free fall, my gut rolling, my body both sweaty and chilled, feeling as if I'd be sick at any moment. Sadly, very little had to do with being in the car, but I'd let him believe that for now. The truth had been gnawing at me for the last day, ever since the doctor had said the words out loud. The words I hadn't believed were possible.

"Sorry," he whispered, rubbing the back of my hand with his thumb, making me feel like a huge jerk for not telling him. "Just a little longer, okay?"

"Yeah." I leaned my head against the cold window and squeezed my eyes closed harder, willing away the sick. February in Michigan meant freezing temperatures, bitter winds, and lots of snow. Phoenix had asked me to brave the weather to look at something, and I was quickly coming to regret my decision to join him on his drive.

When I finally reopened my eyes, my stomach no longer ready to revolt, Phoenix was driving us past an abandoned factory. The hulking steel buildings sat empty and deserted, their walls and roofs rusted and decayed. Something once probably vital to the small community left to die and rot in plain sight.

"What did they make there?" I asked, curious.

"Steel. There's still a mill north of here, but that one closed down a couple of decades ago."

The mill sat on what looked like a narrow river but wasn't. The water flowed calm and flat where I spotted it through the fences, slow but with a depth that drew me. The strait sang to me, pulled me toward it, begged me for help. "It's sick."

"The mill?"

"The water." I pointed across him. "It's polluted and sick. The water is sad. I think it needs me."

Phoenix rubbed my arm and slid his fingers between mine, holding us together. "Yeah, I think it does, too."

He drove past the mill and through a cute little town on the water's edge where old homes and small businesses graced the main street. The water lightened the farther south we traveled; the sadness and call for help lessening. I kept my face turned toward the east and watched it pass, my eyes glued to the small rolls and waves that indicated the motion beneath the surface. I wanted to be in it…to touch the waves and feel that undertow. Especially now, when my inner turmoil threatened to upend my life. I needed my familiar.

It had been a hard transition from living on Lake Michigan, what was more an inland sea than a lake, to the city. Detroit was okay, too gritty and urban for me, but life with Phoenix was good. Calm. And yet the water—the deep strait that ran between Detroit and Canada—just wasn't enough to quench my need. My elemental magick had suffered the past few months, taking me down a challenging path with it. And my little secret wasn't helping anything either.

Phoenix turned toward the water, driving silently. The only sounds in the car were the soft music on the radio and the concrete under the tires. The sun stayed hidden behind winter clouds, the sky heavy and gray. But the water… Oh, the water looked so beautiful as we approached. Deep and dark, drawing me to its icy edge. Enthralling me with its magick. I couldn't take my eyes off it.

After a quick dogleg turn, Phoenix drove us over a short metal bridge. My body perked up at being so close to my beloved element, at being nearly surrounded for even that fleeting moment.

"Is this an island?"

"Yeah," Phoenix said as he made a hairpin turn off the bridge, making my stomach lurch. "I thought you might like being surrounded by water for a little while."

"I love it." I smiled as best as I could, my witch powers settling in a way they hadn't since we'd driven away from the lighthouse where I grew up. "Where are we going?"

"You'll see."

Phoenix drove along the waterfront where huge houses sat overlooking the water. The river side of the street remained empty, though. Protected from development, it seemed. Perhaps so that others could share in the views. And the views were lovely. Or they would be once spring came bursting through the snow and ice. I hoped we'd get to come back when the world was in bloom once more so I could see the green meet the blue. See the sun reflected off the subtle waves.

After a long stretch, Phoenix turned down a wooded street lined with homes of all sizes before turning onto what looked like an overgrown driveway. He followed the icy, rutted path, scowling the whole way. I gripped the door and tried to breathe through my nose and out my mouth, wishing for something to take my mind off the churning in my gut.

Phoenix growled his wolfy rumble, a sure sign of his frustration, as he twisted the wheel hard to avoid a huge hole. "Sorry."

"Don't break my car."

"I'm doing my best."

Finally, he came to a stop. He put the car in park in front of an old stone home. Small and squat, it looked like some kind of cottage you would expect to find hidden deep in the forest. Everything about the property looked brown and dead, but I could feel the life of the place. Could sense the resting plants almost ready to come back. We were close to the water here, and in the spring, this property would be beautiful. I could feel it in the energy around me. The earth was only resting, after all.

"Where are we?"

Phoenix turned off the engine and gave me a smile. "You'll see. C'mon."

He hurried out of the car and over to my side to help me out. That was a nice thing about my mate. He was well-mannered, honestly caring, and always concerned, especially since I hadn't been feeling well. Not that he knew why I'd been so sick. Neither had I, of course. Not until yesterday. I'd known for almost twenty-four hours, and I'd been too afraid to tell him. Not afraid he'd be mad, just afraid he wouldn't be as excited as I was. Because when the shock wore off, excitement and amazement had filled me. But I had no idea if he'd feel the same.

Oblivious to my internal turmoil, Phoenix led me into the old house without knocking, ignoring my questioning gaze. The air hung stale and dusty, the place a bit shadowed as there were no lights and it was almost as cold as it was outside, but the house radiated happiness. It felt warm walking in, as if the structure itself was giving me a hug. The earth gave this place a good energy, something a witch like myself never took for granted. Whoever lived here was very lucky.

Phoenix stood in the middle of the empty living room, looking surprisingly intense. He stared at me, waiting for something—some kind of reaction—but not giving me any indication of what he expected.

"What is it?" I asked, the weight of his stare making me uncomfortable.

He swung one arm out as if displaying the house for some reason, before running his other hand over his hair. "What do you think?"

I looked around the room again. I did like it—the ancient pine wood floors, the stone fireplace on the far wall, the windows along the back showcasing the woods. It was a cute house, happy and calm, with the water close enough to soothe my elemental core in a way I hadn't experienced since I'd moved east. Though I still had no idea why he'd brought me to the place.

"It's nice…charming and calm. It has great energy." I stepped toward the kitchen and shrugged. "Who lives here?"

Phoenix paused, looking ridiculously nervous. He licked his lips and then sighed. "We do."

I gripped the counter, suddenly dizzy, my eyes burning with how wide they must have been. "Pardon?"

"I bought it for you." He stepped toward me, each move slow and deliberate. Cautious. "I bought it for us."

Oh, my sweet, sweet man. He made my heart hurt, made me feel so undeserving of his care and consideration. He made me feel even worse for holding things inside.

"You bought us a *house?*"

"Yeah." He smiled and shrugged, so damn charming and young sometimes. I wanted to kiss that smile off his face, to throw myself in his arms and show him with my body how much he meant to me. But I couldn't.

"You *bought* us a house," I whispered, still trying to wrap my head around it. "You bought us a house on an *island*."

Phoenix grinned and grabbed my hand, leading me to the windows at the rear of the house. He wrapped his arms around my waist and pulled me against his chest, leaning down to whisper in my ear, "Not just on an island, on the water. The river is just past those trees."

I looked out the window to where the dark water of the strait peeked at me through the bare trees. My heart raced in my chest and my mouth went dry. I had no idea what to say or do. How could I keep such a huge secret from him when he was so damned sweet to me? Why couldn't I just tell him?

"You bought me water." I gripped his hand in mine, terrified of letting go. The emotional significance of that physical act not lost on me.

"I did." He cuddled me closer as his lips brushed my ear. "My water witch shouldn't be in the city. I only wish I could have found us something on Lake Erie so you could have more water."

I shook my head, my thoughts spinning. "What about your work?"

He kissed my neck, nuzzling his favorite spot. "It's only a half-hour commute to the denhouse."

"What about money? I'm not working, and now…"

Phoenix didn't seem to notice how I couldn't finish my sentence. Damn it, I needed to tell him, but the words wouldn't come. It was as if they were stuck inside of me. As if the fear of messing up the amazing thing we had together held them at bay. And Phoenix, my beloved wolf shifter, just took it all in stride, not knowing how much his casual generosity was tearing me in two.

"I had a bunch of money saved up," he said, still curling his big body around mine. "And I got a great deal because this place has been in foreclosure for three years."

He spun me around, looking excited but wary. "I wouldn't

have bought it without you seeing it, but you've been so sick and I needed to jump on an offer. I just…I was so sure you'd like it. So," —he grinned— "do you like it?"

"I do. I absolutely love it." I shook my head as my eyes burned, my tears falling fast and hard. "Oh shit, babe. What did you do?"

"What?" He crouched down to look me in the face, gripping my arms and pulling me close. "Baby…don't cry."

Baby. The word felt like a kick to the stomach, making this whole moment that much more intense and painful. Making me feel like such a horrible person for not telling him the moment I found out. For holding this heavy, heavy secret that was as much a part of him as it was me.

"I…I have to tell you something," I whispered.

Phoenix just nodded, looking at me as if he trusted me to tell him anything and we'd be okay. Like there was no doubt for him in us. But this…this was big. This was not something we were ready for, and I had no idea if he'd be okay with the news.

I bit my lip, wanting so badly to just say the words but still having trouble letting them go. Two words was all it would take, and then I could let the chips fall where they may. But this was Phoenix, my red thread, the other half to my soul. If he was disappointed or upset, I'd never get over it. I needed him by my side with this, but I didn't—

"Azurine," Phoenix said, interrupting my spiraling thoughts. "What is it?"

I took a deep, shuddery breath. "I didn't mean to keep it from you. I mean, I knew but didn't know, you know? And then I did know, but not for long, and you were busy last night, and today I kept chickening out, but now, you bought us a house, and I can't go on knowing while you don't know when you bought us a beautiful, perfect little house."

"I'm not following you." Phoenix brushed the hair off my face and smiled at me. "Azurine, you're my mate, my heart. You can tell me anything. So…just tell me."

I felt my lips shake and my eyes fill with tears as I stared at the man I loved. Terrified, but hopeful. And deep down, so damned excited I could hardly breathe.

"I'm pregnant."

The words hung in the air, a physical force or an energy, almost like the moment between a lightning strike and the roll of thunder. The anticipation before the storm. Phoenix went completely still, his body stiff and his face slack. I waited for the words to register, hoping he wasn't disappointed, knowing it was too soon. We'd only met three months ago. And though he was my mate, my red thread, my fated match, it was still so fast. Babies hadn't been on my mind at all, but apparently, my body had other plans. Even with my birth control pills, our little nugget had demanded a chance at life. And damn it, I wanted her to have it.

I knew the moment my words filtered through Phoenix's brain. Instead of a storm, I got a sunrise. His smile blazed, spreading across his face like the light of a new day. Brilliant, bright, and warm, he grinned as he grabbed me in an almost crushing hug.

"Are you sure?" he asked, holding me close, looking at me in wonder.

I nodded, joy and relief rushing through me. Why had I waited? Why had I even worried for a moment? Of *course,* Phoenix would love the idea of having children. The past twenty-four hours melted away, all the worry and the stress and the uncertainty. All disappeared in the light of his smile.

He leaned down, kissing me, owning my mouth with his. His hands on my ass, he pulled me against him. I ran one knee along his outer thigh, teasing him, wishing we could be closer. And naked. But late February in Michigan in a house with no heat was no time to get naked. We'd freeze our bits off.

"That's why you've been so sick?" he asked as soon as he

pulled away.

"Yeah, though I had no idea. I never expected this."

Phoenix dropped to his knees and rested his cheek against my belly. "When?"

"October. I'm due in early October." I swallowed hard, the tears on my cheeks burning in the cold.

"We can't tell anyone," he murmured as he ran his hands over my hips. "Not for a while, and only our closest friends and family at first. Jesus, if word gets out that a shifter and a witch made a baby—"

"We'll figure it out." I ran my fingers through his hair, smiling down at him. "We'll keep her safe."

"Her?" He quirked an eyebrow.

I shrugged. "Witches have witchling babies, and all witches are girls."

"A little girl. We'll have to buy a lot of smoke alarms in case she's a fire witch like Scarlett." His smile turned softer, his hands slowly roaming all over my hips, stomach, and thighs. "But a little boy might be nice, too. We just don't know."

"Not yet. Soon." I smiled down at him, loving how peaceful and happy he looked.

"You have given me such a gift." Phoenix kissed my belly, and then rested his head against my hip bone. His lips moved as if in prayer, his words too soft for me to hear. I ran my hands over his shoulders and neck, up into his hair, settling us in the moment.

Finally, he moved to rest on one knee. He tilted his head back, his eyes bright and the expression on his face making my knees weak. Filled with so much love and hope. I swear, I could see our future as he looked up at me.

"Marry me."

My heart jumped and I grabbed his shoulders. "What?"

"Marry me. Not because of the baby or the house." He pulled a small box from his pocket, fingering the lid. "Marry me because you love me. Because you can't live without me. Marry me because I love you more than I ever thought possible and I never want to be apart from you."

"Marry me because I've been carrying around this ring since Christmas, just waiting for the right time to ask you." He rose to his feet, leaning over me, brushing his lips against mine before he murmured, "Marry me because you love me as much as I love you."

I grinned and nodded, barely able to speak because my throat was too tight. This man, he'd been such a rock of faith and support since the day we met. He had become my best friend and my lover over the course of our short relationship, and now he would become my husband.

"Yes," I finally whispered. I laughed when his grin widened, holding him tightly as he lifted me off my feet. "We're going to be parents."

"I know." He wrapped his arms around me and buried his face in my neck. "I am so lucky to have you. Both of you."

I ran my hands up his back, squeezing him to me, needing his body against mine. "And we're lucky to have you. We're lucky to have found each other."

As he growled, the tug of the water returned. This time it was a bit more forceful, a need for me instead of a want. I closed my eyes and focused on my magick, giving myself over to the elemental side of myself. The water wanted to celebrate, to touch and feel and take part in this day.

"Soon," I whispered. Phoenix pulled back, giving me a quizzical smile. "Everything will come together soon."

And as his lips met mine, as he kissed me in our living room, in our home, on the island I hadn't known existed, all the pieces fell together. This was our true beginning, our chance to have our own family. One we both desperately wanted. The throwaway kid and the orphan.

The family Tackett.

Books by Ellis Leigh

THE FERAL BREED SERIES
Claiming His Fate
Claiming His Need
Claiming His Witch
Claiming Their Forever: A Feral Breed Anthology
Claiming His Beauty

THE GATHERING TALES
Killian & Lyra
Gideon & Kalie
Blasius, Dante & Moira
Blasius, Dante & Moira: Homecoming

About the Author

A storyteller from the time she could talk, Ellis grew up among family legends of hauntings, psychics, and love spanning decades. Those stories didn't always have the happiest of endings, so they inspired her to write about real life, real love, and the difficulties therein. From farmers to werewolves, store clerks to witches—if there's love to be found, she'll write about it. Ellis lives in the Chicago area with her husband, daughters, and a giant dog who hogs the bed.

Find Ellis online at:
Website: www.ellisleigh.com
Twitter: https://twitter.com/ellis_writes
Facebook: https://www.facebook.com/ellisleighwrites